ZACH KRYTON
THRILLER

GREYFIN

JOSH
FRANCIS

Greyfin – A Zach Kryton Thriller (Book #4)

This is the first story that continues chronologically after the Zach Kryton Introductory Series – it is recommended you read this series first.

WARNING: some obscene language

Copyright 2022

Josh Francis

ISBN: 978-0-6487025-3-5 (paperback)

Published by Red Diamond independent publishing

Josh is seeking formal representation

www.red-diamond.com.au/books

Sign up to the reader's group

This story is fictional!

Cover media by Onur Aksoy – Great work Onur!
www.onegraphica.com

Also By Josh Francis

Pegasus – The Zach Kryton Introductory Series (Book 1).

Poseidon – The Zach Kryton Introductory Series (Book 2).

Phoenix – The Zach Kryton Introductory Series (Book 3).

Battle Rhythm – The military-inspired personal planning, discipline and motivation guide (The Camouflage Series Book 1).

Centre of Gravity – The principles soldiers use to think, act and achieve success (The Camouflage Series Book 2).

Under the Pump – Anecdotes of a service station operator.

Follow Us

You can find other publications and join our conversations on social media. This will keep you up to date with upcoming books and allow you to share ideas. Feel free to contribute!

INSTAGRAM

FACEBOOK

AMAZON

Please leave an honest review on Amazon. This helps to tailor and improve the content of what we produce.

Contents

1

Eighty Mile Beach, Western Australia
19°39'27"S, 120°54'54"E
2035 local

The two soldiers laughed as they watched the seagulls fight over the few scraps of food they had thrown down onto the ground. What had started as a free feed for one curious and fearless bird had now turned into a frenzy as his mates decided to also take in the spoils.

Patrolmen John Betts and Terrence Gulpilil sat in their camouflaged, cut down Land Rovers facing Eighty Mile Beach – a long expanse of sand that seemingly extended for miles in both directions. The open top vehicles were perfect for embracing the cool evening air, and they enjoyed looking on as the sun began to set behind the beautifully vast and calm Indian Ocean. Both proud Yindjibarndi men, they were even prouder of their status as soldiers of the Pilbara Regiment, a unit within the Australian Army's Regional Force Surveillance Group – RFSU.

The RFSU regiments were responsible for monitoring the vast swathe of open and remote country that made up the northern part of the Australian continent. Predominantly consisting of reservists, many of its members were from the local indigenous tribes that knew the country intimately, all based on knowledge handed down by generations that went all the way back to the dreamtime.

The two men were actually cousins, and spent every moment they could together; whether it be playing football back home near the Fortescue River, or on patrol in service of their nation.

The rest of the patrol had married up their vehicles in some dead ground to the rear of the beach and had begun their preparations to settle in for the night.

"Having fun, lads?" asked their superior officer as he walked up to the sandy knoll where the two men were conducting the picquet.

"Hi, Boss," said Betts enthusiastically. "Just playing with some of our friends here."

1

Lieutenant Alex Haas looked at the feeding orgy occurring near the front wheel well of the Land Rover. He picked up part of the army issued ration pack the two men had placed on the bonnet.

A young officer in his early twenties, he was not long out of RMC Duntroon, and was now undertaking his first posting as an RFSU patrol commander.

"What did they do to deserve this?" asked Haas, referring to the very average quality that some of the army's ration packs were infamous for.

The two soldiers laughed. They respected their boss immensely. In the Australian Army, if you respected your commander – and if they were amicable to it – you would call them 'Boss'.

Anything else meant that the soldiers still weren't too sure about you.

Haas had come up to the picquet point to ensure all was well as his men settled into their night routine. He loved patrolling the expanse countryside of remote Western Australia, and was somewhat disappointed that they would be returning to barracks tomorrow after their largely uneventful two-week patrol.

A patrol where they had only encountered a few brave travelling tourists and a seemingly endless supply of uninterested emus.

He sat with his soldiers for a while, and they watched as the top lip of the sun slipped slowly under the horizon. The few clouds now reflected the deep glowing orange of the setting sun.

Perfection.

Those moments made any person with an appreciation of nature take a minute to pause and take it all in.

"Okay lads, you have the picquet list there?" asked Haas.

Betts passed it to his boss. It was an improvised roster written on scrap paper that would dictate when each man would take his turn on watch.

Haas smiled.

"Three until half-four. Not bad," he said, handing the list back to Betts.

Haas never cared which picquet timing he had, especially in the middle of the night, as it allowed him to enjoy watching the magnificent stars of the southern skies, unimpeded by the light pollution of the big cities. Other soldiers simply wanted a picquet time that gave them as much uninterrupted sleep as possible.

Every soldier has a theory on which time of the night is best.

He went to walk off when suddenly a faint groaning mechanical wail emanated from the sky towards the southern end of the beach, slowly growing louder as it approached their position.

The soldiers all looked in the direction of the guttural sound, occasionally seeing a glint of light reflecting off of the metallic surface of an object that was struggling to stay airborne.

They watched as a charcoal grey twin-prop plane slowly descended parallel to the waterline.

"Certainly wasn't expecting to see that tonight," deadpanned Haas.

The young officer picked up a pair of binos sitting in the glove compartment of the Land Rover. He placed them to his eyes, slowly twisting the eyepieces in order to focus the glass onto the now landed plane.

"Engine trouble?" queried Gulpilil.

Haas just shook his shoulders.

"Dunno. Can't see any smoke," replied Haas.

They watched as the plane decreased its speed, now taxiing along the perfectly flat sand. The low tide provided a perfect runway for the plane to make its impromptu landing.

"Keep an eye on it," instructed Haas to the two patrolmen.

He moved back down to the remaining vehicles and picked up the satellite band radio. It would give him communications back to their base at Karratha, over 450 kilometres away to the southwest.

"Zero Alpha, this is Emu Alpha One Sunray, over," he said into the radio, as a few of the other platoon members made their way up to the picquet vehicle, curious as to what was happening.

Haas made his report back to base, and then returned up the berm to join what was now a small party of soldiers, all looking curiously at the plane sitting idle up the beach about 600 metres away.

He looked again through the binos, and could see three men standing outside of the plane. The distance made it hard to specifically identify their individual features, but he could tell that one of them was much larger than the other two.

Haas picked up the handset of the VHF radio that sat in the centre console of the Land Rover and pressed the PTT button before speaking into the mic.

"Unknown aircraft, this is Australian Army patrol, hailing you on channel one-six, over."

Further down the beach, standing by the wing of the plane with a now exposed engine, stood a well-built man. Caucasian, in his early forties, and with a large moustache and several days' worth of facial growth, he looked imposing next to his two scrawny Indonesian companions.

"Don't touch that," he said harshly to one of the young men, who was about to pick up their radio to respond to the challenge. "Get back to fixing this thing."

The young man did as he was instructed, and re-joined his companion by the wing where they were trying to find the location of the damaged fuel line. They quietly muttered words to each other in Bahasa, the main language of Indonesia.

The Caucasian man reached back into the plane and pulled out his own set of binos. He quickly scanned the length of the beach, searching for the origin of the radio call that had disturbed their attempts to find and fix the cause of their unscheduled landing.

He quickly found what he was looking for, locating the Land Rover and several men silhouetted against the evening twilight.

"Shit," he mumbled under his breath.

He quickly turned around and again ordered the two Indonesians to hurry up and fix the issue with the engine.

The two young men, sweat pouring from their brows, had identified the problem: a fuel pipe had split and was causing the engine to splutter. They quickly fashioned a short-term solution with some spare hose and electrical tape.

Back up the beach, Haas jumped into the Land Rover and instructed his subordinates to drive towards the plane.

"Let's go and see if we can lend them a hand," he said as he settled into the rear seat.

The seagulls quickly scattered as the engine of the army vehicle kicked into action. They didn't move too far, however, and they quickly returned to the remnants of food left for the pickings after the Land Rover had driven off.

Patrolman Gulpilil eased the Land Rover over the crest of the berm and guided it down towards the beach proper. Both cousins were excited to see some sort of activity after what had been a rather boring fortnight.

Haas held on tight as the young soldier traversed the bumpy berm, before flooring the accelerator just as the tyres gained traction on the firm sand of the beach.

"Jesus, Terry," exclaimed Haas as his grip tightened on the roll bar above the seats, duly concerned that he might fall out.

"Sorry, Boss," replied Gulpilil, as he straightened the wheel and drove towards the plane.

Betts tried to hide his cheeky smile as he looked at his cousin, who had a look of concern on his face that came from almost accidentally throwing his superior officer out of the Land Rover.

Back at the plane, the two young Indonesians were applying the last touches to their patch-up job. The Caucasian man looked back into his binos and up along the beach. He could see the Land Rover quickly approaching.

"We have to go. Now," he demanded.

"We need to face into the wind," said the young Indonesian, pointing up the beach in the direction of the rapidly approaching soldiers.

The Caucasian man nodded. He knew that meant that they needed to take off in the direction of the current threat. He reached into the rear of the plane and pulled out an AK-47 assault rifle. He took a sight picture of the approaching Land Rover.

Crack – Crack – Crack.

He fired off several rounds. The noise startled the younger Indonesian man, who quickly collected his improvised toolkit and raced back to the front of the plane, jumping into the cockpit.

It was obvious that they hadn't expected their passenger to be using a powerful weapon.

Haas was the first to notice the muzzle flashes, which lit up the rapidly darkening evening sky. The *crack-thump* of the AK rounds flew mere millimetres above his head.

"Stop the fucking car," he screamed, ducking down and firmly gripping the shoulder of Gulpilil.

The driver slammed his foot on the brakes, bringing the heavy Land Rover to a rapid halt and kicking sand up, causing Betts to smash his head against the dashboard.

The crack of his nose breaking was quickly followed by the distressing sight of blood pouring down his face and onto the front of his camouflaged shirt.

He let out a loud groan.

Gulpilil exclaimed something in his native language, clearly concerned for his cousin, before reaching for his Steyer rifle. He nervously fumbled with it for a moment, before muscle memory kicked in as he aimed it in the direction of the plane.

Not an uncommon reaction for a young soldier experiencing his first combat action.

He placed the weapon onto 'instant'.

"No, lower that weapon," instructed Haas firmly but in a composed manner, seeking to further assess the situation.

Gulpilil did as he was ordered.

The young lieutenant pressed the PTT button on his radio. The rest of his patrol had heard the gunshots and had already started to move up onto the beach.

"All callsigns, stand fast," he said calmly.

His presence of mind to not immediately return fire displayed maturity beyond his years. He couldn't confidently determine what was happening, and his rules of engagement were somewhat ambiguous about firing upon three men in a grounded plane, even if they had been fired upon themselves.

The Caucasian man stood next to the plane; his AK still raised towards the Australians. He was satisfied that he had achieved his intention of forcing them to pause for a moment.

It allowed the second Indonesian man enough time to close the casing of the engine and hastily join his companion inside the plane.

"Let's go," the Caucasian man said loudly, slowly walking backwards towards the door of the plane.

He kept one eye on the static Land Rover up the beach, and one eye around the top of the sandy berm which ran parallel to it.

He knew the Australian vehicle would not be alone.

Haas instructed Gulpilil to return to their original picquet position, whilst simultaneously calling his signaller forward to the same location.

The young Indonesian pilot switched the engine on, willing the fuel line to stay intact long enough to get them airborne.

The plane spluttered for a moment.

The pilot twisted the throttle, looking over his shoulder at the wing with the previously damaged engine.

"Get this fucking thing up," demanded the Caucasian man, becoming increasingly impatient.

The young pilot's colleague screamed something in Bahasa.

Sweat poured off of the brow of both of them.

Suddenly, the engine kicked in and came to life.

The Caucasian man allowed himself a reluctant smile, nodding at the pilot in satisfaction.

The two Indonesians could barely contain their relief.

Back at the picquet point, Haas had been joined by his signaller, as well as the platoon sergeant, who had driven to the point in their own Land Rover.

"Get me Karratha," he said to the young signaller, who immediately made contact on satellite communications.

By now, and at their sergeant's direction, several of the patrol members had taken up prone positions on the berm and were aiming their rifles at the plane. They held their fire, watching as the plane began to taxi up the beach and away from them.

The pilot was seeking to create enough space to make his take-off into the wind.

Haas finally had success with his communications, and he spoke to the watch officer at their unit headquarters back in Karratha. It was of little use. The watch officer was a corporal who could do little to elaborate on the appropriate rules of engagement. He would never be able to reach the unit CO in enough time to make an authoritative decision.

Haas terminated the call and glared at the plane, which was now making its turn back towards them. He estimated it to be no more than 750 metres away.

He quickly looked at his much more experienced sergeant, seeking the advice of his many years of hard-earned experience.

The sergeant understood that the young officer was seeking advice. He looked back at his much junior boss and smiled.

"Do it, Boss," he said simply with a confident nod of the head.

Haas tried to conceal his smile. The brief action had been exciting, but it had also made him angry. He was keen to prove himself, and not to appear weak in the face of a decisive moment – especially in front of his soldiers.

He believed in the concept that it was easier to ask for forgiveness than seek permission.

He didn't have much time. He gave a set of snap orders, instructing the team as to his intentions.

"Vehicle Alpha, take left side. Bravo, you're right. We drive at them and force them to abort the take-off. Swap Betts out. DO NOT fire unless fired upon. Remaining men, you get the cameras out and grab as many photos as you can, in case we don't pull this off. Questions?"

There were none.

Some of the patrol members quickly helped Betts out of his Land Rover and continued administering first aid. Two other patrol members jumped into the cars, one in each vehicle. Haas also joined them.

The sound of a revving plane engine filled the air as the aircraft slowly commenced moving to begin its take-off.

Haas directed Gulpilil to drive down to the beach, and they were quickly followed by the platoon sergeant's Land Rover. The two vehicles immediately entered a well-drilled assault formation, and as previously ordered by the young officer, started quickly driving in the direction of the plane.

The Indonesian pilot continued to force down on the throttle with one hand, guiding the wheel with his other. His companion said something in Bahasa, pointing towards the other end of the beach.

The Caucasian man was sitting behind them, and propped himself in between the front seats to see what the issue was.

He immediately saw what it was.

Two sets of headlights, at full beam, were coming towards them.

And quickly.

The pilot baulked for a moment.

His much larger passenger reached down to the console towards the throttle, firmly placing his hand over the pilot's and forcibly pushing forward.

"Keep going," he said calmly.

The Australians held firm as the plane continued towards them, quickly gaining speed. The two Land Rovers were no more than ten metres apart, perfectly abreast.

The gap quickly closed, as the machines violently charged towards each other like in a medieval jousting match.

400 metres...

300 metres...

The pilot had the throttle flat to the dashboard, but he still hadn't gained enough speed in the evening's light wind.

200 metres...

"Hold," shouted Haas to his soldiers.

Gulpilil gripped the steering wheel tightly. His eyes with a steeled resolve to get back at those who he held responsible for his cousin's injury.

100 metres…

The Indonesian passenger screamed in Bahasa, ducking into his seat in order to avoid viewing the unfolding scene.

His companion, now sweating even more profusely, pulled steadily back on the wheel.

50 metres…

"Shit," mumbled the sergeant as all of the soldiers tightly grasped a part of their vehicles.

Adrenaline quickly gave way to fear.

40 metres…

The front wheel of the plane raised off of the sand, quickly followed by the rear ones.

"Fuck. Abort," screamed Haas, suddenly realising the lunacy of the action.

The well drilled drivers split away simultaneously, each going in opposite directions just as the base of the ascending plane went tearing between them. They were close enough that the soldiers in the rear could quite feasibly have reached out and touched it.

The Caucasian man quickly moved to the window and looked down at the Land Rovers, assessing to see if they were damaged.

He saw nothing to suggest that contact had been made, which meant there was no damage to the plane.

The pilot let out a deep sigh of relief as the plane continued to gain altitude.

The Land Rovers decelerated and turned back towards where the plane had just taken off. They formed up next to each other.

"Everyone okay?" asked the sergeant, as ever concerned for the welfare of the younger soldiers, even the lieutenant.

They were all breathing heavily, fully aware of what might have been, but otherwise all fine.

Haas stepped down from his vehicle and walked a few paces in front of it, watching as the plane slowly turned north.

He was starting to second guess his decision, realising that someone could have seriously been hurt, until his sergeant walked up next to him.

He could see the young officer was starting to doubt himself. He sought to help ease his superior's concerns.

"It was a fair call, Boss. No one is hurt."

Haas nodded whilst he continued to watch the plane fly away.

He quickly composed himself, and even allowed himself a small smile.

"Thanks, Sarge," he said, lightly slapping his second-in-command on the shoulder.

The two men returned to their respective vehicles.

"You all good, Terry?" Haas asked his driver.

Gulpilil had a look of dismay on his face. He was annoyed that they hadn't been able to stop the plane. Haas squeezed his driver's shoulder, seeking to console the young man.

"Don't worry, we'll report it, and we'll get them," he said reassuringly.

He just hoped that his team had managed to get the photos that would be of critical intelligence value to his higher command.

"Let's get back to the others," Haas said. "We're going to have to inform Canberra."

2

The white Toyota Corolla sedan slowly inched its way up the narrow, windy single laned road as it approached the crest of a small hill. The driver looked across the front of their car, and could see the roof of what appeared to be a single-story house nestled amongst the large gum trees; the only man-made object set at the base of a small mountain which formed part of the Nerang State Forest.

He gently pulled the car over to the side of the road, ensuring it remained out of sight of the house.

"This is the place," said Shane Cavan – known to his many friends simply as Cav.

He applied the handbrake and gently turned the ignition off.

Sitting next to him in the passenger's seat was his long-term friend, Zach Kryton.

"Agreed," said Kryton softly, looking down at the electronic tablet on his lap.

A small red dot was slowly pulsating over a satellite image of the house they were now parked near.

"We still have surprise?" asked Cav.

Kryton exhaled deeply. He thought for a moment.

He reached down to his hip pocket and pressed the small PTT button on his personal radio.

"Zulu One, this is Dingo One. We are at target," he said.

"Acknowledged," came the reply through both of their respective covert earpieces.

The response was from Jonas, running the operation from an undisclosed location.

"Intelligence suggests that the hostage will be tortured, if not killed. You are authorised to conduct a direct action to effect a recovery. Please acknowledge," said Jonas to the two men in the sedan.

"Acknowledged," replied Kryton. "Number of tangos?"

"Expect three," came the confident reply over the radio.

He looked at Cav, who nodded with a wry smile.

"Long arms?" asked Cav enthusiastically.

"Long arms," replied Kryton.

The two men quickly opened their doors, keeping a low profile as they moved to the rear of the car. Dressed in jeans and t-shirts, they otherwise looked like two tourists going for a pleasant drive.

Not an uncommon sight in this part of South-East Queensland.

The afternoon sun was beating down and the humidity level was typically high. Sweat immediately started beading on both of their brows.

Kryton opened the boot of the car. Both men reached in, each retrieving a SIG Sauer MCX automatic rifle. They also placed small chest rigs with body armour on over their shirts, and put ballistic eye protection on.

"Too bloody hot for this," said Cav.

They loaded their weapons and double-checked the status of the Glock pistols that they already wore covertly in their rear hip holsters.

"Okay, what's best?" said Kryton, as the two men huddled to the side of the car away from the road, looking at the electronic table to get an idea of the outlay of the house.

They spent no more than three minutes making a quick appreciation of the environment, and deciding what approach would work best.

"The creek line," they both said simultaneously.

Their plan devised, Kryton placed the tablet back in the car.

"Let's do it," he said.

"Zulu One, this is Dingo One. Commencing our approach now," said Kryton into the radio.

Two bursts of radio static were sufficient enough to acknowledge that their message had been received.

Both men stepped off and away from the car, keeping low to the ground as they moved towards the creek line that ran adjacent to the house.

They worked their way through several strands of rusty barbed wire fencing, and then entered the dry creek bed. Leaves and twigs cracked under their feet, and a lizard scurried away as its sleeping place was disturbed.

They moved swiftly, keeping as quiet as possible until they came to the base of a large gum tree which would afford them some concealment.

They crouched behind it, gingerly looking over the top of the mound at the edge of the creek bed. About fifty metres away was the side of the house. It was an old weatherboard constructed design, with a veranda at both the front and the back. A corrugated iron shed was sitting to the rear in what was essentially the backyard – typical of the houses in the area that often served as homesteads for farmers, or as what appeared in this instance, hobby farmers.

The windows appeared to have been boarded up, or deliberately obscured with curtains.

"No sign of any presence outside," whispered Cav.

Kryton nodded.

"Worst possible time of day to do this, too," he replied to his friend.

He brushed the sweat off of his brow, and ran his tongue over his lips, trying to keep some moisture in his body.

"Got the picks?" he asked Cav.

Cav looked down and placed his hand on the small pouch on the front of his chest rig. He nodded in the affirmative. The pouch next to it held two flash-bang grenades.

Operators always triple-checked their equipment before they went on a job, but there was just something reassuring about running a hand over your equipment just before you intended to utilise it.

"Okay, I lead. With Me?" said Kryton.

Cav placed a hand on Kryton's shoulder and squeezed it softly.

"With you," he replied.

The two men stood and quickly exited the creek, making a beeline for the rear corner of the house. Their rifles were raised at shoulder height, ensuring that the full 180-degree arc in front of them was being covered for any potential threats.

They quickly made it to the corner of the house, and now stood back-to-back, still covering their arcs.

Kryton gently pivoted the top of his body and looked around to examine what was at the back. There was a small set of stairs leading up to the rear of the house. From where he was standing, it appeared that the windows at the back were also boarded up.

The house looked exactly like somebody was trying to hide something. Possibly a meth dealer – or something more nefarious.

Kryton tapped on Cav's shoulder to get his attention. He pinched his fingers together and twisted his wrist. Cav nodded. It was the sign that they would make a soft entry by picking the locks.

Cav turned, and Kryton gently squeezed his shoulder.

As per before, the two men rapidly and quietly moved across the back of the house, before proceeding up the stairs, taking up a position against the back door.

As was the case with most Australian houses, there was a flimsy metallic framed door with a fly screen outside of the main door.

Cav moved his rifle to the side of his body, which was held up by its sling. He quickly scanned the door for wires or any potential booby traps – a precaution learned as a legacy from their experiences in Afghanistan where the Taliban would often place IEDs against entry points of buildings.

Finding nothing, he gently grasped the handle of the first door.

It opened easily.

Kryton turned and raised his weapon at shoulder height to cover Cav, who now squatted next to the main door. He attempted to turn the round handle.

Locked.

Cav reached into his pouch, taking out two small metallic lockpicking devices. He inserted them into the lock, fiddling with them for about ten seconds as sweat continued to pour from his brow.

Suddenly, he heard the soft click he was hoping for.

He allowed himself a small smile as he placed the picks back into his chest rig and retook possession of his rifle. He stood up and grasped the handle of the door, looking at Kryton.

The intelligence operative looked over the sight of his rifle at Cav and nodded back.

With one swift and smooth continuous motion, Cav turned the handle and pushed on the door, stepping back as Kryton quickly moved past him as he entered the house. Cav quickly followed.

They commenced their room clearing drills. A practice they had completed incalculable times in training at Holsworthy Barracks as young soldiers, as well as globally on numerous real-world missions.

They exited the small laundry which was the first room, before entering the kitchen. Across the other side was a man sitting at a table

14

reading a newspaper, unaware of the intruders that were now in his presence. A small pistol sat on the table in front of him.

Kryton walked quickly towards the man, who looked up in shock.

The man went to grab the pistol, but was instantly stopped by the two rounds that Kryton put into his chest, causing red matter to spray across the table.

The Australians continued moving. They entered the dining room, which was adjacent to the kitchen, and split into the corners as per their well-practiced drills. Suddenly, another man, this time armed with an AK-47, stormed into the room.

Kryton and Cav fired simultaneously into the target, causing him to fall over a small coffee table before coming to rest as a motionless lump in the corner at Kryton's feet.

The two operators slowly moved up the hallway, clearing the rooms one by one.

"Hmmmpf," came a loud groan from a room down the end of the hallway.

Cav led Kryton as they moved slowly towards the origin of the noise. They gently approached the room and stopped a few paces short of the doorway. They had cleared the rest of the house, and they knew there was still one tango unaccounted for.

Well, at least one that they knew of.

There was no need for hand signals anymore; their presence in the house was now obvious.

"Go," said Kryton.

Cav stormed the room, immediately turning to his right and clearing the long end of what appeared to be the master bedroom.

Kryton entered mere milliseconds after Cav. He trained his rifle along the short end of the room until he was inside enough to turn rapidly to assess for any threats in the main part of the open clearing.

Cav had literally stumbled into a man armed with a pistol. Both of them were too close to engage with their weapons, and a struggle quickly ensued.

Kryton made an appreciation of the rest of the room, which was devoid of any furniture except for the far corner where he saw a man armed with a knife kneeling next to a woman tied up on a chair. He recognised the hostage immediately.

It was Jo.

The tango went to place the knife against her throat whilst simultaneously leaning closer to his prisoner.

Kryton aimed his rifle straight at the man's throat and pumped six rounds straight into him. The incapacitated man slumped onto the floor.

He quickly turned to see Cav engaged in some scrappy unarmed combat on the floor with his own opponent. Kryton attempted to train his rifle onto the other tango, but couldn't get a clear shot.

He lowered his rifle and let it hang from its sling. He looked down at Jo, who had tape across her mouth and who was also watching the scene unfold on the ground. He tilted his head to the ground, almost amused by the amateurish scuffle at his feet. He looked back at Jo.

"So, should we just let them keep going?" he asked her humorously.

Jo let out a small groan from behind the tape. Kryton reached down and pulled it off of her mouth. She stretched her jaw out, embracing the ability to breathe properly again. She scoffed at his question, looking at him in an unimpressed manner.

"Perhaps untie me first," she replied.

A large siren rang out from outside.

"EndEx. EndEx," came the voice through the earpieces, quickly followed by the same words over a megaphone from the rear of the house.

Cav and his opponent ceased fighting. Their weapons were strewn across the room. Kryton looked down at Cav, who looked back at his friend with a determined grimace.

"Well, look at the size of him," Cav protested, as he and his much larger opponent slumped against the wall, breathing heavily.

"All callsigns, RV at the control centre," said Jonas over the radio.

Kryton asked the man who he had shot if he was okay. The young man removed the glasses that had protected his face. He looked down at the large red mess across his neck and chest, where the simunition rounds from Kryton's rifle had impacted and splattered red paint.

"I'm good, sir," said the young man, excited from having played his part as a role player for the exercise.

Kryton nodded.

"And what about me?" asked Jo, trying to undo the improvised knots of rope that were tying her hands behind her back.

"Oh, sorry," said Kryton, reaching down and offering her assistance to get to her feet.

16

After releasing Jo and helping Cav to his feet, the three of them walked back through the house. The other role players were tidying themselves up, and several other plain-clothed people had entered the house, placing all the furniture back into position.

The role players had also been utilising simulated weapons. But they had been no match for the professional operators who had just defeated them in their successful hostage recovery.

Kryton smiled as he observed the young men rubbing their chests.

Simunition rounds were essentially no different to a paintball when hitting the body, and they particularly hurt when hitting at close quarters.

The three of them walked outside and down the stairs of the house. Jonas was waiting for them by the corrugated iron shed with a megaphone in his hand. He waved them over with his free hand, and they followed him into the shed.

Inside, they found several people standing around a large desk, all talking and pointing to various maps and paperwork. A suite of television screens covered the far side wall, which displayed live images from inside the house from the CCTVs which had been hiding in the corners of the various rooms.

Jonas pointed to a couch tucked away in the corner of the shed next to what appeared to be an old 1970 Holden Commodore. It had obviously seen better days, though there was enough of it remaining for someone to take on a restoration project.

Kryton, Cav, and Jo slumped into the couch.

A young analyst brought each of them over a bottle of water, which in the Gold Coast humidity didn't stand a chance against the thirsty trio.

They were exhausted.

They had finally concluded a three-day Operational Readiness Exercise – or ORE – which had seen them complete numerous tasks across South-East Queensland in order to consolidate training, and to prove their new capability as 'mission ready'.

An ORE in which none of them had slept for nearly seventy-two hours whilst they had undertaken a seemingly endless number of special operations and intelligence focused missions. Surveillance; reconnaissance; intelligence gathering; and, counter-intelligence operations. All culminating in simulating the recovery of a captured intelligence operative in a hostile foreign environment.

The sort of ORE where even the role players required a top-secret clearance.

The junior army intelligence officer trainees probably didn't mind a day out of the classroom so that they could play the 'bad guys'. The welts that would soon form on their body might make them regret their decision to volunteer for it, though.

Kryton poured some water onto his hand and rubbed it over his face. The military had a saying: 'Train Hard. Fight Easy'. If that was true, and based on how he felt at that moment, any future action should be a walk in the park.

Jonas walked over and kneeled down next to the three of them.

"The bosses are just reviewing that last activity. We'll wrap it up here and head back to Canungra," he said.

Apart from being a picturesque small town nestled into the valleys of the Gold Coast hinterland that drew tourists on weekends, Canungra also hosted the Australian military's intelligence school – a secure and secretive facility that was tucked inside a training area that had been used to prepare soldiers for jungle warfare since Vietnam.

"Thanks, mate," replied Kryton, trying to conceal a yawn.

Cav had already started to doze off, much to Jo's amusement.

"He's had a big day!" joked Kryton quietly.

"Bugger off," mumbled Cav, his eyes staying closed.

Kryton quietly observed the gaggle of people inside the shed. Although they were dressed in relaxed casual, they were some of the most powerful people in the national security bodies of both the Australian and US governments.

Standing at the desk in the middle of the shed alone was the Australian Director-General of Intelligence; the US Director of National Intelligence; each nation's respective Special Operations Commander; as well as a collection of civilians from the wider military and intelligence communities.

"Let's leave them to it," said Kryton as he stood up, tapping on Cav's knee to rouse him.

The three of them walked outside. Kryton was comfortable mingling with the brass, but even he had a threshold for the amount of personnel with stars he was willing to share a room with.

3

The sun had already started descending behind the dense, tree-covered mountains when the three of them returned to the barracks from where they had set up an improvised base of operations. They drove through the main gates and followed the windy road across a river that led them up to the side of a hill. Here among the trees, they reached a set of demountable buildings which were heavily secured by a large fence adorned by multiple strands of barbed wire.

A compound within a compound.

They all looked forward to getting some sleep. It had been a long six months.

After Kryton had stopped the assassination of Vice President Kendrick – an assassination attempted by a man who had actually been working with Kendrick in a coup attempt against the United States – it had been decided to form a highly skilled and highly classified unit that could stop the events that would disrupt global peace and harmony.

The type of events that would have significant catastrophic consequences if allowed to occur.

President Jack Lang had personally signed the directive authorising its creation, along with his Australian counterpart, Prime Minister Ed Kernahan. It had been decided that two incredibly close allies would work together to initiate the formation of such a unit.

Kryton walked into a small communications office and found US Navy SEAL Clay Dalton with his feet up on a table watching a television screen. The images on the screen appeared to be CCTV footage from inside the house earlier that day.

The American looked up and smiled at seeing his Australian counterpart.

"Hey man, I see it went well."

"We could have used your help," lamented Kryton.

"Sorry, man. They killed me off. I got four of them first, though," proclaimed Dalton proudly, motioning to another screen which was replaying footage of some other close-quarters combat from earlier in the exercise.

Kryton leaned over the table next to Dalton and examined the screen.

"Hmm…there were *only* four."

Dalton pushed Kryton away fervently, scoffing as he did so.

"How's your chest?" asked Kryton, laughing.

Dalton rubbed the part of his body where a Chinese bullet had collected him in Timor-Leste.

"It's at about ninety per cent."

Kryton nodded, pleased to see his colleague had healed, remarkably well considering the wound he had received. The two had become firm friends since meeting six months earlier.

Kryton went to walk out of the room.

"Zach – do you think they'll let me be involved," asked Dalton, with genuine concern in his voice.

Kryton stopped in the doorway and looked back at the American. He felt genuine empathy. He knew first-hand exactly what it was like to get thrown on the pile because of a combat-related injury.

"I don't know, mate. Who knows if any of this will get off of the ground. Try not to think about it. Tomorrow's a rest day, and I did promise everyone a swim."

Dalton nodded, sat back up properly in his seat, and returned his attention to the screen. He would continue to review the footage of his efforts well into the night.

It was the hallmark of every good special forces operator – to always be looking to improve; to learn from mistakes; and, to get better.

Kryton walked into the evening twilight as Jonas pulled up in an army owned Toyota Camry Hybrid.

They nodded to each other as they walked to a larger room, which had served as their planning centre for the exercise. The walls and desks were covered with maps, drawings, sketches, and an assortment of data and photos.

Inside they found Cav and Jo sitting at a table, sipping coffee and discussing the activities of the past few days. The two men joined them, grateful for the cups of coffee that Jo had prepared in anticipation of their arrival.

"So," said Cav, "How did we go?"

Jonas adjusted his chair and opened his black leatherbound folder. He looked down at an assortment of notes.

The other three looked at him curiously, as if they were about to receive their high school term report.

"Well, they seem pleased," said Jonas simply, referring to the thoughts of the high-ranking observers who had been at the shed watching the exercise unfold live on television.

Kryton furrowed his brow and looked at Cav, then back at Jonas.

"Pleased?"

Jonas shrugged empathetically. He understood their desire to know if the last six months had been worth the time and effort.

"The brass is heading back to Canberra tonight. They will make their recommendations to our Chief of Defence Force and the Chairman of the Joint Chiefs respectively, and then up to government."

Dalton walked into the room and took a seat next to Kryton. The Australian quickly briefed him on what Jonas had just said.

They sat there for a moment in acceptance. Another day of not knowing wouldn't make a difference. It was the standard mantra – hurry up and wait!

They had done their bit. It was now in the hands of the gods.

Only a few very select people had been briefed into the tightly held compartment of the developing capability. Only the most senior officials from the military and intelligence communities of both countries were aware of what was being created. Even the role players in the exercise had been told a cover story – something along the lines that they were supporting a general special forces training exercise.

But they had not passed yet.

There were some exceptionally high standards to be developed and implemented. And even then, every day would be a test of an individual's willingness, resolve, and commitment.

"Go and get your heads down. Your time tomorrow is your own, and we'll RV back here at 0900 the day after," said Jonas.

They stood from their seats but were interjected by Jonas.

"Oh, we've also been asked to come up for a codename for this unit, should...when, perhaps... we get across the line."

The team looked at each other.

"What are we using so far?" asked Dalton.

"Well, officially this is Project 1942, in recognition of our two nation's efforts together during the Second World War in the Pacific against the Japanese."

"We'll give it some thought," said Kryton sarcastically, thinking it of little relevance.

Dalton returned to his videos, whilst Jonas and Jo decided they were keen to call it a day.

Kryton and Cav stood in the open air for a few moments, looking at the stars. The temperature and humidity had reduced significantly, and it was going to be a lovely evening.

"Pub?" asked Cav.

Kryton smiled.

"Sure. Why not!?"

The two men took their car back to the accommodation area of the barracks, where they had been staying for several weeks. It was of standard Australian military design – a three-level dormitory with shared bathrooms.

"Give me five minutes. I'm going to have a quick shower," said Kryton as they opened the doors to their adjacent, individual rooms.

Cav nodded.

As he returned to his room after his shower, Kryton could hear the most god-awful chainsaw like noise coming from Cav's room.

He just shook his head and smiled.

A few minutes later, his own head was on the pillow and off in dreamland for the night.

4

Kryton and his team spent a quiet day recuperating on the magnificent sands of Surfer's Paradise. Clay Dalton easily embraced the stereotypical Australian experience of sand, sun, and surf, and attempted to charm the local females with his Texan drawl.

Without success.

"They turn you down?" asked Jo as Dalton walked back up to their little spot on the sand, his last attempts to woo a voluptuous blonde in the surf zone having failed.

The SEAL sat down and sighed. He wasn't defeated just yet.

"You're creeping them out, bro," murmured Cav, lying on his back with his hat protecting his head from the sun.

"No, I'm not," protested Dalton. "How else are you supposed to meet people?"

Jo looked at Kryton, who shrugged his shoulders and gave an understanding nod.

She just shook her head.

The four of them sat quietly and let the cool afternoon breeze wash over them.

They had trained exceptionally hard over the past few months and deserved their very small amount of time off.

It was out of their hands now. The senior special operations and intelligence officials who had been observing the final exercise would make their recommendations. The final decision to give Project 1942 the green light would rest equally with the Australian National Security Committee of Cabinet, as well as its US counterpart, the National Security Council.

Kryton looked out at the magnificent blue ocean. Several surfers, both experienced and novice, plied their skills as the southerly breeze made for perfect conditions. Children played in the waterline with their parents, whilst couples walked hand in hand along the beach, getting lost in conversation and not having a care in the world.

He breathed in deeply, and slowly exhaled – a meditation technique he had learned that enabled mindfulness.

He thought about the past six months, and back to that day when Jonas had fetched him from the martial arts mats at the RMC gymnasium. He thought about how the army had been so ready to be done with him because of the injuries he sustained in that IED blast in Kabul. He thought about the hypocrisy of the bureaucracy which allowed him back only when *they* needed something from him.

What fickle masters we work for, he thought to himself.

Any doubts his own hierarchy maintained about his ongoing capabilities had been quickly quashed. Something to do about a personal request from the President of the United States to have him part of the project.

He looked across at his colleagues, who were laughing as they talked about nothing in particular.

He was glad to be working with Cav and Jo again; two good friends, each from a different time throughout his distinguished career. And Clay Dalton, the amicable American sailor who he had grown to respect like a brother.

He laid back down onto his towel, covered his face with his arm, and smiled.

There was nowhere that he would rather be.

Just as he started to doze off, a loud, shrill beeping came from under the crumple of clothes that were piled in the middle of their spot. Kryton sat upright and reached down to take the call.

He listened intently.

"Yep. Okay. We're at the beach," he said incrementally into the handset, as the others looked over to see what the fuss was all about.

Kryton looked back at them with a serious look on his face as he continued the one-way conversation.

"Roger that. We'll be there in sixty minutes."

He finished the call and looked over at the others.

"What is it?" asked Jo.

"Sorry, team. Our time off is over. Jonas wants us back ASAP."

"Guess they made their call," said Cav, as they all stood from their comfortable spots on the sand and turned their attention back to work.

A little under an hour later, the sand mostly removed from their bodies and now wearing clean civilian attire, the team were sitting back in the main conference room of their secure compound at Kokoda Barracks.

Not a bad effort time-wise in the end, considering the afternoon traffic around Surfer's Paradise, and which Kryton had made up for on the windy roads of the valleys of the hinterland. The Queensland Police Service and the army typically had a good relationship. One Kryton was confident he could call upon should he have had his driving abilities questioned by a young rookie constable looking to make their daily quota.

After a few minutes, Jonas entered the room, leading a small procession of very senior looking people. Kryton recognised a few of them from the final exercise at the farmhouse.

"Room," said Jonas firmly.

The military personnel responded instinctively, standing up in response to the call to attention. Jo followed suit – the civilian in her having never quite adapted to military protocol.

"I thought they were all going back to Canberra," whispered Cav, leaning over to Kryton.

Kryton just shrugged. He was no wiser than his friend was as to why the senior members of the military and intelligence community were now standing before them. Jo and Dalton also had confused looks on their faces.

Two men walked to the front of the conference table, whilst the other VIPs took seats, or a standing position, facing the front of the room.

A tall man walked over to Kryton, extending his hand in a friendly greeting.

"Nice to see you again, Sergeant," said Bradley Kingston, the US Secretary of Defence.

"Nice to see you, too, Mister Secretary," replied Kryton, warmly shaking the secretary's hand.

They were joined by another man of similar age and height.

"You know Minister Williams," said the secretary, introducing his counterpart, the Australian Minister for Defence, to Kryton and his team.

Once the brief informalities were concluded, the two VIPs cordially asked the team to resume their seats. Secretary Kingston began speaking.

"Okay, I'll get to the point. POTUS and the PM have signed off on this concept. Project 1942 is a go," he said, a satisfied smile on his face.

Kryton tried to hide a sigh of relief. Cav and Dalton were less restrained, sharing a fist bump as was typical among special forces operators.

"Congratulations. I know how much effort has been put into this," added the minister.

"We wanted to inform you personally. We've been monitoring your progress, and POTUS has certainly been interested in your efforts," said Kingston.

For the next minute, the two VIPs said a few salient words of encouragement. Nothing too ostentatious or of a political nature. No patriotic motherhood statements. Just enough to demonstrate that they had an understanding of the nature of the work that came with special operations, and the inherent risks that went with it.

Kryton was impressed with their level of knowledge of the project. He respected any politician that was brief, factual, and humble.

"I don't need to stress the secrecy surrounding all of this. Even our own public schedules have stated that we're conducting policy meetings in Canberra today," said Williams, pointing to himself and the secretary.

Good to know they can keep a secret, Kryton thought to himself.

Almost as soon as they had arrived, the VIPs left again, taking their small entourage with them, and leaving Jonas to continue briefing the team. He sat on the edge of the table at the front of the room. The four team members relaxed in their seats.

"Well done," he said simply.

For Jonas, too, it had been a long six months. The bureaucracy among the senior levels of government, the intelligence community, and the military, could be brutal at the best of times. Trying to navigate through all of it among the highest levels of not only one but two nations, albeit allies, was nothing short of impossible.

Yet, he had worn that burden, and the outcome they had achieved was nothing short of miraculous.

"However," he continued, "although the ORE was a success, the fact is we're only now at the start line. This concept is still experimental in nature, and we will be judged on our successes as well as our failures."

Kryton and Jo nodded knowingly. Being from the intelligence trade, they knew better than most that intelligence operations never received credit when successful.

But their failures were always widely known, and well criticised.

The offset of operating in the shadows.

"Good news is, we are now the most classified entity within each of our respective arsenals. We'll have every resource openly available to us – NSA, CIA, ASIS, JSOC…you name it," briefed Jonas.

Cav and Dalton sat a little more upright, interested in what Jonas was saying. As special forces operators, they were used to receiving every possible advantage in order to go into battle. But even to them, this seemed like an unprecedented level of facilitation of equipment and support.

It made it clear just how significant this project was to the head shed.

"The best possible analysts and operators from each of the major agencies and military units have been selected, and they will be briefed in and seconded to us as required," added Jonas.

"Where will we be based?" asked Cav.

"Ostensibly, at HQJOC down near Canberra. This will allow reach back to all the systems and support we may require. But this will be a highly mobile operation. We'll go where we're needed, and when we're needed. We demonstrated that when chasing Kendrick's thugs across the Pacific. Like I said, every possible resource."

The four seated team members looked at each other, sharing confident nods. It was now that it started to seem very real.

Jonas stood up from his seat at the edge of the table and walked over to a moveable whiteboard that was on a set of wheels. He took up a marker and walked around to the other side.

"Our missions will come directly from the combined national security committee which has been formed, consisting of senior US and Australian representatives," he said as he wrote something on the other side of the whiteboard, facing away from the others.

Jonas placed the marker back down, placed one hand in his pocket, and leaned on the whiteboard with his other arm.

"So, what *will* they expect from us?" asked Jo, seeking just that little bit more clarification as to their purpose.

Kryton spoke up. He had been part of it from the start, and intimately understood the reasoning.

"The world isn't any better as a result of all the wars and sacrifices of the past 20 years. If anything, the wars in Afghanistan and Iraq have taken the focus off of everything else. China is rising; North Korea is still a threat; Russia is still doing what Russia does."

"And that's only the state-level actors at play," added Jonas, "not to mention all the crazies out there that have their own warped agendas and causes."

He stood upright.

"Our role, as two great countries who have done more than their fair share globally to keep world order, is to protect our national interests, and to promote the concepts of peace and harmony," he said.

Kryton chuckled at the bold statement made by his friend. That was a politician's statement.

"But…in layman's terms," he continued as he looked at Kryton, smiling, "our job is to stop bad guys from doing bad shit. A highly skilled team of operatives; capable of covert and clandestine actions; tasked to stop the worst threats from carrying out those catastrophic world-changing events before they happen. Wherever. Whenever. This is intelligence-driven special operations. As unique and pure as it gets."

Kryton allowed himself a small smile. Now that sounded more like it. That was something he could get behind.

Jonas looked across at the faces of the team. He sensed they were getting comfortable with where things were at. He could sense they were eager to get on with the job. Keen to prove themselves.

Like all professionals are.

"Now," said Jonas, changing the tone and pace of the discussion, "Jo has been good enough to come up with the winning suggestion for our code name."

He moved back over towards the whiteboard.

"We wanted something simple. Something to reflect our mission, and who we are. Now, considering that we are designed to remain unseen, in the shadows, and only appearing at the last minute to cause devastating effect, I thought this suggestion was highly suitable."

He flipped the whiteboard over. The four of them looked at the single word written on it.

Greyfin.

Dalton smiled and nodded. Anything maritime sounded good enough to him.

"Why not!?" he said.

"Simple is not the only reason I like it," said Jo, gesturing towards Jonas.

Jonas returned the smile, reached into his leather folder, and pulled out an A4 sized colour photograph.

28

"A surveillance photo that Jo managed to get during one of the training serials when you two were pretending to know how to surf," he said.

He placed it down in front of Cav and Dalton. Kryton leaned in closer to have a look as well.

The very clear picture showed the two men each sitting on a surfboard, just out past the surf break at Surfer's Paradise. Not a care in the world between them, and posing to allow Jo and Kryton to test their covert long-range image collection skills.

More significantly, however, it showed the very grey – and very large – shark fin protruding from the water only a few metres away from the two oblivious special forces operators.

Dalton's face turned ashen white.

"A hammerhead, probably," said Jonas. "But quite possibly a tiger."

Kryton stood up and patted the SEAL on the shoulder.

"What's wrong, frogman? Scared of a little fish!?"

Dalton continued to stare at the photo in disbelief as the others stood from their seats.

Jonas had one final word to say before they left.

"Just keep one thing in mind. This isn't *Mission:Impossible*. This is real life. Our operations will be critical. They will be 'no fail' missions. We have to make this succeed."

Cav furrowed his eyebrows.

"But I want to wear a mask like Tom Cruise," he moaned jokingly.

"You should probably always wear a mask over that head," said Dalton, winking at Cav as they walked outside.

The two shooters traded several slow and friendly blows, mimicking a fight and laughing as they did so.

Kryton and Jo followed them.

They stopped for a moment and enjoyed standing in the sunshine. The afternoon was starting to settle in, and the sun would soon be behind the mountains of the hinterland.

Jo looked up at Kryton.

"I…I just wanted to say thanks," she said appreciatively.

"What for?" he asked.

"For this. For bringing me on."

He smiled back at her, surprised by her graciousness. He paused for a moment. He wasn't really sure how to respond.

"No worries," was all he could muster. "It wouldn't be the same without you."

She nodded and started to walk away.

"You know, Jo," he said, suddenly finding words and slowly walking towards her, "whatever was between us, whatever was in the past…it doesn't…it doesn't change the fact you're one of the best intelligence operators I've worked with."

She smiled sheepishly, caught off guard by his flattering comments.

They both looked over at Cav and Dalton, who were now play fighting over the set of car keys.

"Perhaps don't thank me just yet," he said, motioning to the two men.

She laughed.

"So, shall we get a gym session in?" she asked hopefully.

He shook his head, declining her offer.

"I can't, sorry," he said simply. "I have to visit an old friend tonight."

5

Kryton slowly eased the government-owned Toyota Camry into the long driveway of a beautiful two-story house situated near the top of Tamborine Mountain.

He drove past several rows of vines – the grapes having all been removed several weeks earlier during the late spring harvest.

Several large palm trees adorned the top of the driveway, and he drove up next to a twin roller garage. He opened the door, pulling his tired body out and standing next to the car.

He looked up at the house. It was a Queenslander style design with large stilts holding up the majority of the second level. Ostensibly, houses of this design were built to allow elevation in the event of the floods that parts of coastal southern Queensland frequently received.

However, it appeared that this design was to afford the house an even better view across the hinterland valley and down to the sprawling Gold Coast skyline.

Kryton enjoyed the magnificent view for a moment. The last parts of the setting sun were reflecting off of the top of the tallest buildings, and the lights from those same skyscrapers – mostly hotels – started twinkling in the evening sky.

Kryton heard a noise to his left. The shifting of gravel under tiny feet. He looked over his shoulder and saw a medium-sized dog – a black and tan coloured kelpie – looking at him curiously.

"I wouldn't move too suddenly," came a firm voice from the balcony of the second level of the house.

Kryton tilted his head and looked up at the voice. A tall, bearded man, with whitish blonde wavy hair, was looking back down at him. A sly smile on his face.

Kryton looked back at the dog.

31

He narrowed his eyes as the canine made a grumbling noise.

A classic Mexican standoff. Two equally matched opponents, not prepared to give any quarter.

Suddenly, Kryton smiled, clapped his hands twice, and hunched down on his heels.

"C'mon, boy," he said playfully.

The dog ran over at top speed, almost knocking Kryton over as he launched himself at the soldier like someone reuniting with a long-lost friend.

The bearded man nodded approvingly, before turning away and walking back into the house.

Kryton stood up, walked over to a set of stairs, and ascended them up to the balcony, the dog playfully jumping up and down as he did so.

"Graham. Here," instructed the man to the frisky dog as Kryton reached the top of the stairs.

Like a well-drilled soldier, the dog left Kryton, ran over to the man, and sat dutifully by his left-hand side.

"He remembers you," said the man as the two warmly embraced.

"He's a good judge of character," replied Kryton.

They walked inside to a kitchen table top, where two empty glasses sat neatly next to a freshly opened bottle of Lagavulin scotch whiskey.

Kryton took a seat on a barstool at the bench as he watched his long-time friend and mentor pour two generously sized servings.

Adam Johns – the former senior enlisted Australian military intelligence soldier – had worked with everyone and anyone within the special operations and intelligence communities, on both sides of the Pacific, as well as with the fabled MI-6.

As Kryton's first-ever boss when he had joined the intelligence trade as a junior soldier, he had taken the young paratrooper under his wing and taught him enough to survive in the shadowy world of special operations intelligence.

If Kryton had had a distinguished career, then Johns' own was of almost mythological standing.

There were rumours that he had been in Iraq well before the Special Air Service Regiment – SASR – had clandestinely crossed the border in early 2003, and that the intelligence he had acquired from sources very senior in the Iraqi regime had ensured coalition success in the western Iraqi desert, denying Saddam the opportunity to fire missiles into Israel and thus preventing a wider regional conflict.

All just rumours, though, and only known amongst the tightest of circles within the coalition intelligence community.

Johns passed Kryton the glass, and the two men toasted to nothing in particular.

"It's a nice night," said Johns, motioning for Kryton to join him on the balcony.

They walked outside, looking down over the valley and across to the ocean many kilometres away.

The two men sat down in comfortable chairs next to a small rock fire, which served aesthetic rather than practical purposes in the still warm evening.

Kryton took a sip of the whiskey and allowed himself a moment to fully appreciate the view. It was the most relaxed he had felt since the beginning of the intensive six months of training and preparation that had gone into the formation of Greyfin.

For the next hour, the two experienced intelligence operators shared stories and reminisced. The tranquil surroundings of the hinterland meant that they were left undisturbed to reflect on different, perhaps even better, times.

"…and then the CO had to tell you to stop bashing up his shooters," said Johns as the two men shared yet another war story, laughing so loudly it could probably be heard down by the coast.

Kryton sipped at his drink, struggling to swallow it between the fits of laughter. Although he was actually somewhat embarrassed by the story himself, his friends relished sharing the infamous tale of the day an SASR soldier tried to push in line in the mess at the special forces compound in Tarin Kowt.

And how a young intelligence analyst – a mere support staff member – had taken umbrage to it, politely informing the experienced special forces operator that there was in fact a queue.

When the shooter offered the young man the opportunity to take up the issue outside, he found a willing opponent. When only the analyst returned inside after the unmistakable sound of a body hitting the floor, the look on the faces of the mostly beret qualified personnel eating their lunch was priceless.

"Not only did the commandos who we were working for think it was funny, even a few of the SASR guys quietly congratulated me. That bloke wasn't the most popular guy in that squadron," said Kryton.

They both continued laughing as Johns topped up the glasses.

They sat comfortably in silence as the dog started making whimpering noises in his sleep. Kryton looked down at the peaceful canine and smiled.

"Are you still instructing at the school?" asked Kryton.

"A few days a week, mostly during the basic and officer courses. It supplements my pension. I think they just want to keep an eye on me. That's what happens when you know where all the bodies are hidden."

"Did the investigators question you about the war crimes stuff?" asked Kryton.

Johns just shook his head.

"Nah. Funnily enough I actually wasn't there when any of that stuff happened, so I wasn't called in thank goodness. What a shit show," he lamented.

In late 2020, the ADF released a report on an internal inquiry into war crimes committed by Australian special forces personnel in Afghanistan.

To say that the inquiry was damning was an understatement. But more damning were some of the immediate responses by the Australian government; apportioning blame without proper investigation by federal law enforcement authorities, and stripping awards and citations from units who had played no part in the allegations.

The all too familiar response within the ADF – group punishment for the actions of a few.

The entire saga had left a bitter taste in the mouth of the thousands of military personnel who had served in the various special operations task groups during the war. A legacy of bravery and personal sacrifice tarnished by the disgraceful actions of a very few rogue operators.

"Makes you wonder if all the shit we did was even worth it," said Johns, staring into the distance.

"I hope so," replied Kryton softly. "I mean, I wouldn't be going back into it if I didn't believe in something."

Johns looked over at his protégé and gave a wry smile.

"You were always the idealist in a realist world. I admired that about you, maybe because you always kept faith in what we were doing," he said.

"And you didn't?" responded Kryton.

Johns just shrugged. Despite whatever stoic façade he might have portrayed to others, he often spent many sleepless nights trying to reconcile in his own mind the things he had seen and done throughout

34

his career, and whether the price people had paid in blood had been worthwhile.

Sometimes he thought it best to not consider such questions, lest the answers prove hard to fathom.

"So, what have they got you doing?" asked Johns.

Kryton placed the glass on the small table between the chairs and leaned in towards Johns. He looked over his shoulder – a subconscious practice indicating somewhat sensitive topics were about to be discussed.

"They're going to try a grey ops unit again," he said. "A joint military and intelligence team."

Johns just scoffed and rolled his eyes.

"This again!?" he said, sipping at the whiskey.

Johns was right to be pessimistic. Australia didn't have the best history of conducting deniable operations in the grey zone. ASIS had utilised a paramilitary force once, but a very public training failure in the early eighties had seen that concept shelved.

Kryton nodded. He understood his mentor's pessimism, and sought to elaborate on the new project in order to ease his concerns.

"We're doing it with the Americans this time. I have a few SEALs and analysts from the CIA, as well as our own people from SOCOMD and The Firm. It's actually a rather strong team."

Johns looked at Kryton with an air of doubt.

"Are you sure you still want to play this game? You've been lucky a few times now. That can't last forever."

Kryton thought for a moment, recalling the way he had been treated by the army when they first told him that his services were no longer required.

"Yeah. I need to finish it on my terms. To feel like I did something worthwhile, after all that has happened."

Johns altered his position in his seat, looking at his friend sympathetically. He knew how Kryton felt…and why.

"Zach, you didn't get Mick killed. It was an IED. No one could have known it was there," he said reassuringly.

Kryton breathed in deeply. He just stared into the distance. He had still not fully come to terms with the death of his best friend in Kabul in the same IED strike that had led to his own career demise.

A suicide strike caused by a double-agent in the Taliban that had once been an ADF intelligence source Kryton had been the handler for; who had ultimately decided that his allegiances were to martyrdom rather than the cash payments that were being secretly paid to him for intelligence.

"You were cleared of any wrongdoing. You can't let that be your legacy," added Johns, always the purveyor of sage wisdom.

Kryton raised his head and looked at Johns and smiled.

"It won't be. I promise."

Johns grasped the bottle.

"Another?" he asked.

"No…I better get going. I'm using a Defence car, and with my luck, the MP's will be waiting out front of the barracks with the breath tester."

Even the most secretive of military units could find themselves facing the wrath of an eager young military policeman ready to enforce the often-ambiguous set of military laws – one of which was no drinking alcohol when using military property.

The two shared some more small talk as they went down the stairs and over to the car. The dog joined them, now well rested and keen to play some games.

"Next time," said Kryton, gently patting him on the head.

Johns and Kryton embraced again. They had both enjoyed the evening, and had relished the opportunity to be in the company of someone they didn't have to obscure their work or lives with. Someone who understood what the other had experienced, and could offer an ear of support.

It was the tried and tested way that soldiers had conducted their own psychological therapy for centuries – over a bottle of good booze and in the company of like-minded people.

Johns placed his hand on Kryton's shoulder.

"Just watch your back. They *will* hang you out to dry if it goes wrong. Just look at this inquiry that's going on. Only you know who you can trust."

Kryton nodded. He jumped into the driver's seat, closed the car door, wound down the window, and fastened his seat belt. He looked up at the house, then back at his mentor.

"I know where to come if I need a hand."

6

The team sat in their seats making small talk amongst each other. Nothing of an intelligent nature, just mostly, as they say in the military, 'smack talk'.

Jonas entered the room; a leather folder and several folded maps under his arm. A serious look covered his face, which quickly caught the attention of the team.

"What's happening?" asked Kryton.

Jonas placed the materials down on the desk at the front of the room. A bead of sweat rolled down the side of his face. Even though it was not yet mid-morning, the humidity was setting in, and his perspiration was aided by the uncomfortable shirt and tie he was wearing, though he had allowed himself the luxury of loosening the collar and rolling the sleeves up.

He looked up, and slowly smiled, indicating that this would be a good brief.

"We have a job!"

The four team members sat a little more upright and looked at each other. Now they would have the opportunity they had been training so hard for.

Jonas shuffled some paperwork and then activated a video projector at the front of the room. He tapped a few keys on a laptop, and an image of a map of north-western Australia projected onto a large screen.

Jonas cleared his throat and commenced his brief.

"Last Saturday evening, a platoon from the Pilbara Regiment were conducting an evening picquet in the vicinity of Eighty Mile Beach," he said, pointing to the location of the beach highlighted on the map.

"A plane landed on the beach, seemingly in distress, but when the platoon commander and several of his men went to offer assistance, they were fired upon by what is believed to be a man with an automatic weapon."

"Believed to be?" asked Dalton.

"They couldn't quite tell from the distance they were at from the plane when they were fired upon, and it was dusk, so visibility was poor," said Jonas.

Dalton nodded, letting Jonas continue the brief.

"Three men were identified by the platoon. One believed to be a Caucasian man, whilst the other two appeared to be Indonesian."

When Jonas pressed the button on the remote control in his hand, the map on the screen was suddenly replaced by a picture of the plane on the beach. He pressed the button several more times, scrolling through the images that had been collected by the soldiers of the RFSU platoon.

"Did they fire back?" asked Cav.

"No," replied Jonas. "The young subbie erred on the side of caution to begin with, but then got all cowboy and decided to try and prevent the plane from taking off."

He showed the team a grainy video, which wobbled in the style of the *Jason Bourne* movies. It had been filmed by the platoon members at their picquet point, and showed the two Land Rovers manoeuvring at speed towards the accelerating plane.

"What the actual...?" said Dalton, his jaw-dropping.

"Yeah, several weeks isolated in the outback makes you do some stupid things," said Kryton.

"Obviously," replied Dalton, still amused at what he was seeing on the screen.

They continued watching the footage, each gasping in disbelief as they watched the plane barely scrape over the Land Rovers as it took off.

Cav looked at Kryton, his eyes widened in amazement.

"Wow," he mouthed softly to his friend.

Jonas turned off the video.

"Okay. The platoon reported that contact, and from then onwards the plane was able to be intermittently tracked north, all the way to the island of Bali," he said, now showing the map on the screen again.

The team continued to pay close attention, but continued to wonder how this might be of importance to them and their role.

"It sounds just like a black flight that almost got caught," observed Kryton.

"Black flight?" asked Dalton, leaning over to Jo.

"Drug runners who sneak into Australia using small planes. There are numerous airfields in that part of the country, and most are left unwatched and unprotected," she informed him.

"Perfect for smuggling drugs in from Asia," added Jonas.

"So how is this a job for us?" asked Kryton, sensing the more relevant details of the brief were still to come.

Jonas pointed the remote control at the projector and pressed the button, making a new image appear. It caused Jo to gasp. It wasn't that she couldn't handle pictures of a dead man with a bullet hole where his left eye once used to be, it's just that she wasn't expecting it.

"Early on the morning of that same day, a man was murdered at the workers' huts at the Fortescue River mine site. Several witness reports indicate that a plane, similar to the Cessna our RFSU friends encountered, landed at a nearby airfield several kilometres from the mine."

"A drug sale gone wrong?" suggested Cav.

"Well, that's the story being sold to the media at the moment. The incident with the plane and the RFSU patrol on the beach is not yet being made public."

Kryton knew that it wasn't a drug sale gone wrong. Not if they were being called in.

"He's obviously someone important," he said.

"Yes, he is," replied Jonas, again changing the image on the screen.

A personnel file, clearly marked *TOP SECRET* at the top, appeared on the screen. A passport-style photo was in the right-hand corner, showing the same man as the previous image, but from a time when his face was a little more intact.

"The murdered man was ostensibly named Peter Wilson, a nuclear scientist who was working on a uranium production project."

"Ostensibly?" queried Jo.

"His real name was Sergei Volkov," continued Jonas. "Volkov was living here under international diplomatic protection. According to our ASIS LO, he and his family were granted protection here five years ago."

"What was he hiding from?" asked Kryton.

"Apparently, he made some enemies inside the Russian government. He was top of his field in nuclear development and advancement, but started questioning some of the influences that the FSB and the military were under from non-state actors within Russia."

"Russian mafia?" asked Kryton.

"Maybe," replied Jonas. "He took his concerns to the Americans, and was granted asylum in exchange for details on the Russian nuclear program."

"And they hid him here in Australia!?" said Cav. "I didn't even know we did that sort of thing."

"We've been doing it for decades," said Kryton. "You'd be surprised how many IRA informants and defectors were tucked away here with their families in the seventies and eighties."

"Volkov was allowed to work in the private sector, helping develop our own uranium management and enrichment processes. From all accounts, he did what he was told, and led a very low-key life," said Jonas.

"So, this was an assassination?" asked Kryton.

"And *this* is why it's a job for us. That's what we have to find out. The key question is: how did whoever did this know that Volkov was here? The Americans are concerned, and want to know ASAP if any other persons under protection have been compromised. I'm looking to get more intelligence about any related links."

Jonas paused for a moment to allow the information to sink in. Each team member scribbled some notes in their personal books, and asked Jonas to scroll through the images back and forth to help consolidate their understanding of the situation.

He picked up and handed Kryton the leather folder he had brought in with him.

"This is the intelligence pack our support team has created."

Kryton placed it on the table in front of him and opened it as the others huddled around him to see the contents inside.

"RAAF air traffic control tracked the plane to a beach near Denpasar. Indonesian police have detained two Indonesian men, and are currently holding them in custody," continued Jonas.

"And the other bloke?" asked Kryton.

"That, we don't know. Your task is to go to Denpasar and interrogate the Indonesians, and to try and pick up the trail of the Caucasian man."

"Any CCTV from the mine site? Any details from witnesses?" asked Kryton.

"We've looked into it, but there's no real security out at those places. Their assumption is that no one will go out to the middle of nowhere to try and steal a massive dump truck."

The team continued to listen to Jonas' brief as they pulled apart the materials in the folder.

"Have any of the agencies been able to identify who he is from the photos?" asked Jo, the analyst in her thinking creatively.

"Not yet, but our team are on it. You'll be updated as the intelligence becomes clearer."

Kryton looked closely at the image of the Caucasian man standing by the plane. It was a grainy photo, but he could tell that the man was of intimidating size and stature.

We find you, we get our answers, he thought to himself.

7

The plain white Gulfstream jet's tyres briefly squealed as the rubber touched the hot tarmac after the long flight from the Australian mainland.

Kryton looked at Cav, who was curled up in the seat opposite him. His colleague was fast asleep – a sleep that had commenced even before the plane had even taken off from Brisbane Airport nearly eight hours earlier. Cav had even slept through the quick fuel stop in Darwin.

He'll sleep anywhere, Kryton thought to himself amusingly.

He shook Cav on his shoulder, waking the shooter from his slumber. Cav yawned, rubbing his eyes and looking around, seemingly confused by his surroundings. It was hardly every day that he got to take a private jet whilst undertaking his duties. He recalled Jonas' words back at the post-ORE briefing: 'every available resource'.

Not a bad way to get around, he thought to himself.

He quickly remembered where he was, and what they were there for.

"Good kip?" asked Kryton.

Cav looked back at his friend and smiled.

"You know it," he replied jovially, now fresh and eager to get to work.

Kryton laughed, and looked out of the window as the plain-clothed RAAF pilot eased the plane into an obscure corner of the apron.

If they thought South-East Queensland had been warm, then the extreme humidity of the Indonesian archipelago made that feel like a refrigerator in comparison. They were glad to have worn loose, lightly coloured clothing, consisting of chinos and short-sleeved collared shirts.

Kryton and Cav walked down the stairs and moved over to a black Toyota SUV with diplomatic number plates where a young female was waiting for them.

"I'm Zach, and this is Shane," said Kryton, introducing himself and his partner to the young Australian representative from the local Consulate-General.

"I'm Emma Watkins, welcome to Bali Mister Kryton," said the young diplomat in her most respectful voice.

She was well dressed in a beige skirt with a light blue collared shirt.

Kryton smiled as he shook her hand. He assessed that she couldn't be more than 23 or 24 years of age. Probably not long out of the Department of Foreign Affairs and Trade graduate training program. It was likely her first posting overseas.

As far as she was concerned, Kryton and Cav were just run of the mill Australian Federal Police – AFP – agents; essentially the equivalent of the American FBI. She would likely assume that they had probably been sent in on a short-term mission that required someone of a certain skill and experience.

The two men jumped into the back of the SUV. They embraced the chill of the vehicle's air-conditioning. If anything, it was freezing. Kryton guessed that the young girl hadn't been in Indonesia for very long, and she was probably still acclimatising to the local weather conditions.

"I've been asked to give you this," she said, motioning to a hardened black suitcase sitting in between the two seats in the back of the SUV.

She handed Kryton a key, and he opened it up and looked inside.

Inside he found two Glock pistols, each with a concealed holster and two spare magazines. Kryton passed a weapon and its associated items to Cav, and they cleared and loaded the weapons as Watkins drove off from the apron.

The planning session after the brief from Jonas had gone long into the afternoon, and finally a plan that involved Kryton and Cav going to Bali undercover as Federal Agents had been approved. However, they didn't have the time to source their weapons before they were on the plane.

The US Consular Agency in Bali had assisted with that one.

Kryton then pulled out a sealed envelope, which was heavily bounded in tamper-evident seals. He ripped them open and took out several stapled pages with a lengthy amount of information and associated images on them.

"Updates?" asked Cav, as Kryton took in the detail within the document.

43

"Yep," murmured Kryton as he read over the intelligence update compiled in Canberra, and sent via encrypted signal to the CIA representative at the Consular Agency, which had then been handed to the Australians.

The update provided no further information as to the identity of the Caucasian man, but it did give some detail about the plane and its likely owners. It also displayed a mugshot of each of the two detained Indonesians. Both of them couldn't have been much older than the young girl driving the two operators through the streets and away from the airport.

"They look shit scared," observed Cav as Kryton handed him the document.

"That will prove useful," said Kryton.

"I've been instructed to take you to the POLRI station in the middle of Denpasar. Your suspects are being held there," said Watkins, using the abbreviation for *Kepolisian Negara Republik Indonesia* – the State Police of the Republic of Indonesia.

"Good," replied Kryton.

He looked out of the window. The morning traffic was now congesting the narrow streets, and motorised scooters, pedestrians, and small cars alike bustled to find any gap available in order to get to where they needed to go.

As was typical among the streets of South-East Asia, might was right, and there was order to what otherwise looked like chaos.

******

Approximately twenty minutes later, the SUV pulled up in front of the main POLRI station in downtown Denpasar. Kryton and Cav jumped out, adjusting their concealed weapons and taking in a deep breath of humid outside air. Both men started to sweat immediately, but it was bearable.

"We'll call you when we need a pick-up," said Kryton to Watkins, standing at the driver's side window.

He handed her the key to the briefcase. She would ensure the materials were returned to a secure safe back at the Consulate-General.

"No worries," she replied, keen to wind the window back up and avoid letting all of the precious cool air escape.

44

Kryton watched as she manoeuvred the large vehicle away from the curb and back into the bedlam of the local streets.

They walked to the guarded gate of the POLRI station and presented their AFP badges. A young male policeman, impeccably attired in dress uniform, checked his clipboard and could see that the arrival of the two Australians was expected. He spoke some words in Bahasa into a phone, and then pressed the button to open the door to allow them access inside.

Kryton and Cav walked inside the main foyer of the station. The walls were adorned with images of POLRI officers performing duties with happy local citizens, as well as the 'wanted' posters of those citizens who would probably rather the police didn't catch up with them.

The tiled floors and wooden furniture were typical of many Indonesian government buildings, and the photo of the President of the Republic of Indonesia held pride of place above the main desk. The air-conditioner was working beautifully.

Even though the locals might be acclimatised to the humidity, it didn't mean they had to put up with it unnecessarily.

"Who are we meeting here?" Cav whispered to Kryton as the two stood in the foyer, both looking at the unmanned main desk.

Kryton was about to respond when a loud clanging noise drew their attention to a door at the side of the foyer. Once opened, a diminutive, middle-aged officer walked through, smiling broadly in the direction of the two visitors.

He, too, was impeccably dressed, with badges and medal ribbons adorning his shirt. Kryton always admired the way many militaries and police services across South East Asia ensured that their personnel wore meticulously tailored custom fit uniforms.

"Mister Kryton? Welcome," the man said in reasonably good English.

Kryton raised his hand and walked over to the officer.

"Selamat pagi pak. Terima Kasih," said Kryton, speaking Bahasa to greet the commander of the station and thank him for his warm welcome.

Kryton shook the hand of the much shorter man firmly but respectfully, before introducing Cav.

"My name is Kompol Siswo Legowo," said the officer, matching the name Kryton had read on the intelligence pack back in the SUV that indicated who they should expect to meet at the station.

Kompol being somewhat akin to the western police rank of inspector.

"Please, please, come this way," said Legowo, motioning the Australians through the door he had just come through.

Kryton and Cav followed the senior policeman up a long hallway and into his office. Similar to the foyer, his walls were adorned with framed promotional images of POLRI in action, as well as a large corkboard with various notes and images on them. Kryton saw several pictures of what appeared to be the officer's family on the desk.

A plaque hung on the wall behind Legowo's desk, which had both the POLRI and AFP badges on it; possibly a gift from a joint training activity, or even a memento from the terrible terrorist attack at the nightclubs in nearby Kuta in 2002, where several bombs shattered the innocence of the peaceful tourist island, killing over 200 people, including 88 Australians.

The AFP and POLRI had worked extensively in the aftermath of the attacks, forging a close working bond that had ensured many of the attackers were brought to justice.

Legowo sat in his large leather chair. Cav had to conceal a chuckle. The station commander's small stature looked almost comical set against the oversized chair, and reminded him of the scene in *Return of the Jedi,* where the emperor lectures Luke Skywalker from a similarly oversized chair.

Cav composed himself as Kryton gave him a disciplinary glare. Legowo sat forward as a young constable entered the office with a tray of tea. The three men took a sip, before Kryton got straight to business.

"Thank you for seeing us, sir. We're keen to talk to the men you detained over the weekend. Has the Consulate-General briefed you on what happened in Australia?"

Legowo nodded, before pulling open a desk drawer and removing a manila folder. He placed it in front of his guests, who shuffled forward in their fold-out seats before opening it up to look at the contents inside.

Kryton shifted through the file within it, which contained several sheets of paper that included the arrest report of the two detainees. It also contained their mugshots.

He recalled the mission brief back in Australia, which had included the photos taken by the RFSU patrol. Their long lens surveillance cameras had been perfect for capturing the images, and Kryton was satisfied that the mugshots in the file before him were of the same men who only a few days ago were standing by a plane on a remote beach in Western Australia.

"Wayan and Nyoman," said Legowo, biting into one of the biscuits from the tea tray.

"Are they brothers, sir? I mean, based on their names," asked Kryton.

Legowo smiled, impressed with Kryton's understanding of Balinese family cultural naming practices.

"Very good, Mister Kryton. Yes, they are brothers, and local hooligans. We know they have affiliations with Laskar Bali."

"Laskar Bali?" asked Cav.

"A sort of crime group. The local version of a bikie gang," answered Kryton.

"How did you detain them?" he then asked Legowo.

"They crash-landed their plane near Double Six Beach. It's in a very popular tourist area. We assume that they ran out of fuel before they could reach a more discreet airfield further inland," replied the station commander.

Kryton looked back down at the images in front of him.

"And it was just the two of them you detained?" probed Kryton.

"Yes. My men were on the scene very quickly, even though it was early morning."

Kryton smiled at the station commander, before looking back at the file. He felt that the inspector was being genuine in his responses, but he couldn't be sure just yet.

"Where has your questioning led you so far?" asked Cav.

Legowo reached over and took the file, flicking through some of the pages which were all written in Bahasa.

"They have stated that they were smuggling machine parts across the local islands," he said, handing the file back to Kryton.

"Machine parts?" queried Cav.

"Yes. Various mechanical items, such as for refrigerators and televisions, are smuggled into Indonesia all the time, in order to avoid custom taxes. From there they get transported to our many islands, where they are sold cheaply to locals, but still at great profit to the smugglers."

Cav nodded, interested in what he was learning.

"We were going to transport them to Kerobokan prison when your people requested to question them. I was surprised to hear that they had flown from Australia before crashing. What were they doing there?" asked Legowo.

"Well, that's what we're here to find out," said Kryton, deliberately avoiding sharing too much information with Legowo.

It was still too early to place his trust in the so-far engaging and friendly police officer.

"We'd like to question them, with your permission of course," said Kryton.

"But of course," replied Legowo with his now ubiquitous smile.

There was a loud knock on the office door, and a young constable entered and spoke to his boss in Bahasa so rapidly that even Kryton struggled to fully understand what he was saying.

Something about an important matter that needed his attention, or words to that effect.

Might need a refresher in the lingo, Kryton thought to himself.

Legowo excused himself and followed his subordinate out of the room.

"What do you think?" asked Cav, leaning into Kryton so close that it was almost a whisper.

"They don't know about the Caucasian guy," said Kryton.

"Maybe he wasn't on the plane when it landed here," suggested Cav.

Kryton shook his head.

"No. The RAAFies tracked it from just after it left the WA coastline, and it didn't make any stops."

"Long flight!" said Cav.

"Drug smugglers often carry extra jerry cans with their aircraft, and fit-out their planes so that they can refuel from inside it mid-flight. It allows the smaller planes that are harder to detect on radar to travel further."

"How creative," mused Cav. "Should we tell them about him?"

Kryton thought for a moment. There seemed no good reason not to; but it also meant that the two detainees hadn't told the POLRI about him either during their questioning, otherwise Legowo would have mentioned it.

Which meant that they were protecting him. Or that they were scared of him. It was also possible the entire local POLRI was in on it. A less likely scenario, but nothing could be discounted this early on.

Either way, Kryton wanted to question the detainees to further gain the information they needed to continue chasing the man down.

"Okay, I'll question them here. You go and look over the plane and see what you can find in it, along with whatever evidence the POLRI guys have recovered," Kryton said.

"Roger," replied Cav.

Legowo returned to his office, profusely apologising for the interruption.

"Not at all, sir," said Kryton, "I'm sure you're a busy man."

Legowo sat back down in his chair and re-focused on the matter at hand.

"So, how can we be of assistance?"

"Where is the plane now, sir?" asked Kryton.

"It's still where it landed, and is being secured around the clock by my men. We're having trouble finding a crane big enough to remove it. One of the wheel struts snapped on landing, and the beach is too narrow to conduct a take-off anyway."

"Would you mind if my colleague here took a look at it, as well as at anything you might have found inside?" asked Kryton, hoping that there wasn't any formal paperwork or requests that needed to be submitted.

"Yes, no worries," replied Legowo enthusiastically, using an idiom that suggested his vocabulary had been influenced by the myriad of Australian tourists that visited Bali each year.

He picked up the handset of his desk phone and called in his shift sergeant. A well-built man in his early thirties soon entered, and Legowo spoke to him in English, instructing him to give Cav every support that the Australian wanted.

Cav introduced himself to the sergeant, excused himself to the inspector, and then went to leave the office. He turned around to look at Kryton, and placed his thumb and pinkie finger to the side of his head.

49

"Phone?" he mouthed to his partner.

Kryton nodded, confirming that they would update each other via their respective mobiles.

Kryton watched as Cav followed the sergeant out of the room, and then turned his attention back to Legowo, tapping his finger on the manila folder.

"If you don't mind, sir, I'd like to have a chat with these two."

8

Kryton sat down in a basic foldout metallic chair opposite Nyoman. The young man appeared nervous with this large Australian sitting at the table opposite, staring straight at him.

He held his hands tightly together, trying to stop them from shaking, and doing everything he could do to avoid direct eye contact.

"Do you speak English?" asked Kryton softly.

Nyoman looked up at Kryton, then lowered his head.

"Oi. Look at me," said Kryton sharply and loudly.

This made the young Balinese man jump in his seat. Even the junior POLRI officer standing in the corner was startled.

"Do you speak English?"

Kryton already knew the answer. Legowo had already briefed him, and most Balinese were bilingual, if not trilingual, with many speaking English, Bahasa, and Balinese. He needed to see if the man was going to start lying straight off of the bat.

"A little bit," said Nyoman shyly.

"Mungin kitab isa Bahasa?" said Kryton in a more friendly manner, suggesting that the young man might prefer to speak Bahasa.

Kryton wasn't intending to make this an interrogation, but rather an informal chat. He had deliberately chosen the second brother to speak to, as he believed the younger of the two would be more likely to open up to him.

Nyoman looked up, surprised to hear the white man speaking the local language so well.

"English is fine," replied to young man, starting to feel a little more relaxed.

"I'm with the Australian police," said Kryton, deliberately avoiding introducing his name. "We need to know what you were doing in Australia."

"I was just helping my brother fly the plane; we were collecting machine parts from Australia. We can make good money for them," replied Nyoman, sticking to the story they had already been telling POLRI.

Kryton sat forward in his chair, tapping his fingers on the table. He was now close enough to Nyoman to make the smaller man start feeling uncomfortable again.

A classic tactic used to keep the man both fearful yet relaxed enough to be free in his answers.

"I know that's not true. You flew with a European type man. What would you say if I told you that he killed a very important person in Australia?" said Kryton.

Nyoman looked up; a genuine expression of confusion appeared on his face. Kryton looked straight back at him. Cool, calm, and collected. Not even a blink.

"No. No. We just got told to fly the plane. We didn't kill anyone," pleaded Nyoman, suddenly changing tack as the stakes instantly became higher.

Kryton let the man sweat for a moment.

"Did you help him kill the man?" he asked.

"No, no. We just flew him to an airfield. It was in the middle of nowhere. He told us to wait while he went away for something during the late hours of the night," said Nyoman, strenuously proclaiming his innocence.

"Why did you land on the beach?"

Nyoman started breathing heavily, and was almost hyperventilating. The fact that his questioner knew about the issues they had during the flight, and who was now proposing that he and his brother were used to help carry out a murder, caused him to panic.

"Please. We did not kill anyone. The engine was old and the fuel line was not working. We had to land to fix it. The big man shot at the people on the beach. We don't shoot at people," Nyoman stuttered, continuing to protest his innocence.

Kryton sat back in his chair, observing the young man closely and looking for any subtle signs of a lie.

A subtle move of the hands, or a twitch of the eye. Sometimes people were just nervous, but very few could remain nervous and confidently lie to a trained professional without being noticed.

"It's okay. I *do* believe you," said Kryton calmly. "I need you to help me find the man who did conduct the murder, though."

He sat back in his chair and removed a folded piece of paper from his shirt pocket. He opened it up and placed it in front of Nyoman.

"Is this the man that flew to Australia with you?"

Nyoman looked down at the piece of paper. On it contained one of the surveillance pictures taken by the RFSU patrol.

"Yes. This is him," he said, his heart racing and all sorts of scenarios – most of them bad – running through his head.

Kryton took the paper, folded it again, and returned it to his pocket.

He reached out and touched Nyoman on the arm, comforting him.

"The police here think you might have been smuggling drugs," said Kryton, motioning to the junior POLRI officer standing in the corner. "However, I don't think that you were. If you help me, I think I can convince them that you were just helping your brother out."

Nyoman's eyes widened even further. He was right to be scared. The punishment for smuggling drugs into Indonesia was frequently death.

The Balinese man started sweating even more profusely.

"Please, we were not smuggling drugs. I will help you, whatever you need," he said frantically, now much more scared than before.

Kryton stood up and moved his chair around so that he was sitting next to the young man. He looked up at the POLRI officer.

"Can we get some water?"

The young officer nodded, then dutifully left the interrogation room.

"Just relax. It's going to be okay. I just need you to be honest with me. Okay?"

He allowed Nyoman to sit and continue trembling so that he could appreciate that the Australian was indeed trying to help him.

The POLRI officer returned to the room with a bottle of water. Kryton opened it and handed it to Nyoman. He took a sip, some of it spilling down his shirt.

"Yes, yes. I will help however I can," said Nyoman.

For the next twenty minutes, Kryton went over every possible detail with the young man: the instructions that he and his brother had received; the very little information that they knew about the Caucasian man on the plane; and, most importantly, the details of the location of the Laskar Bali hideout where they had planned the mission, and which they hadn't told the police about to this point.

A simple bluff – telling him that POLRI suspected drug trafficking – had convinced Nyoman to be more forthcoming about who had accompanied them on the flight.

Kryton thanked Nyoman and left the small room. He felt he had obtained all the information that he was going to from the young man.

He stood outside the interrogation room for a moment, recapping in his own mind the additions to the slowly building intelligence picture. He felt no need to question the older brother, Wayan.

The next lot of questions needed to be directed to someone else.

"What did he tell you?" asked Legowo, pulling Kryton out of his thought bubble.

"I think he might be a lesser player in this. My information obtained suggests that there might have been a third person on the plane," said Kryton, deciding to further inform his Indonesian counterpart, but not completely giving away what he actually knew separately from his questioning of Nyoman.

"Nyoman has also given me the name of a person he said was organising the flight. The man is named Rachmat Aryanto. Do you know of him?"

"Yes, we know of him," Legowo said as he stroked his wispy thin moustache, thinking for a moment.

Kryton was concerned that the senior police officer might feel usurped by the fact the Australian had been able to elicit more information in twenty minutes than his team had in the few days they had been detaining the two brothers.

He sought to quickly bring him back onside, just in case.

"Sir, I'd like to request *your* support to detain Aryanto so *we* can see what he knows," asked Kryton politely.

Legowo motioned for Kryton to follow him up the hallway of the police station. They walked through a doorway and entered what looked like an operations room. Modern looking desktop computers sat on the tables, being manned by officers. Radios squawked in the background, creating a bustling cacophony that was familiar to Kryton.

Legowo walked up to one of the seated officers and spoke briefly to him. The man tapped on his computer, entering details in what appeared to be a database. A profile picture appeared on the screen.

"This is Aryanto," said Legowo, pointing at the screen. "He's a local gangster, often involved in drugs. He has some connections to larger Javanese crime groups."

Kryton looked closely at the image. The man appeared to be in his mid-thirties, of short but solid build, and had a scar across his left cheek.

"How easy will it be to go and pick him up?" asked Kryton.

Legowo paused before replying.

"The Laskar Bali den is in a bad part of Denpasar. I'd have to gather a team qualified in rapid action and riot control."

"Will it cause issues for you if we detain him?" asked Kryton, acknowledging that the station commander – and by extension his family – probably had to deal with threats from local crime entities on a daily basis.

Legowo shook his head firmly.

"No," he replied, smiling. "We will be *very* happy to arrest him."

Kryton nodded, impressed by the commitment of the man.

"How many days will it take to organise your team?" he asked Legowo, expecting that it would require a frustrating amount of formal paperwork and administration to organise.

The seated officer laughed. His superior gently squeezed his shoulder, a sign that his response was a lapse in discipline that although perhaps justified, was nonetheless impolite. Legowo tried to hide his own smirk. He walked over to the wall where a large map of Denpasar hung. Kryton joined him.

The station commander mumbled a few things under his breath, conducting a quick CONOPS in his head. He looked up at Kryton.

"Ninety minutes," he said confidently.

Kryton's jaw almost dropped to the ground. He almost had to laugh at himself, embarrassed at his lack of understanding of local law enforcement procedures.

"Ah, good. That would be good," he said, still feeling a tad foolish.

******

Sixty minutes later, Kryton stood out at the rear of the POLRI station, engaging in mindless conversation with a young officer who was enjoying his smoke break. His phone vibrated in the pocket of his cargo pants.

"Excuse me," whispered Kryton, pressing the button on his encrypted mobile phone and placing it to his ear whilst moving to a more discreet part of the compound.

"Cav?" he said.

"Yeah, mate. I've had a look at the plane. What a piece of crap! I'm surprised it made it this far."

"Find anything useful?" asked Kryton.

"No. It's pretty empty. Anything they might have had they took away with them. There are just a few empty bottles of water. I've spoken to a few of the locals, but they either don't know anything, or they are too scared to say anything."

Kryton thought for a moment. That meant that the Caucasian man had an AK-47 still. If he was held up with Aryanto, it would be a threat to the raiding assault force. He felt relieved when he realised that he could tell Legowo about the threat by saying that Cav had been told by some random local that they saw a man leave the crash site carrying a rifle, as opposed to having to admit that they had been holding back information from the Indonesians.

"What about your end?" Cav asked.

Kryton kicked at some dirt.

"I have a lead to that gang Legowo mentioned before. It's probably the boss of the kids who flew the plane."

"And their companion?"

"I'm not convinced they know who he was. I've got a name though: Rachmat Aryanto. He's like the local leader of the gang. We're going to go and grab him and see what he knows. Legowo is forming a team to conduct a raid. Apparently, it's in a dodgy part of town, and these blokes have been known to pick a fight with police when it suits them," said Kryton.

"Nice one. You want me back there?"

"No. Keep asking around there. You might find someone more willing to talk. Try some of the Aussie tourists, too. Don't be afraid to flash the badge around. We'll RV back at the station," briefed Kryton.

"What time are they going in?"

Kryton looked down at his watch, doing some mental arithmetic on the fly.

"About forty minutes from now."

9

Laskar Bali hideout
Denpasar, Bali
1310 local

Kryton sat in the front passenger seat of the undercover POLRI Toyota Camry hatchback, observing the hideout of the local Laskar Bali group, which was tucked away in the residential neighbourhood near Imam Bonjol Road. The house was on a street that was only a ten-minute drive from Legowo's police station, and was well secured with a metallic gate and large concrete fences.

More of a compound than a house, it was the perfect place to avoid the prying eyes of anyone seeking to look inside.

Like most urban Indonesian environments, the streets were narrow and the housing tightly packed, with drainage pits running adjacent to the roads. Rubber cables hung loosely over the street, taking electricity to the local houses and commercial estates.

An untidy design, but effective nonetheless.

Kryton was about fifty metres away from the front of the compound, and could see through a small set of binos that POLRI would have their work cut out for them penetrating the front of the building.

He was impressed with how quickly Legowo was able to form a team to raid what was essentially a fortified compound, drawing upon officers from across the district who had been trained in conducting this type of activity.

The police radio in the console squawked as the various teams indicated that they were almost at their designated form-up points. Kryton softly adjusted the volume button, lowering the noise so that anyone outside of the Toyota wouldn't get too curious.

Legowo had briefed the POLRI team that they were to detain Aryanto so that the Australian guest could further question him.

Kryton quickly ran through the current situation in his head.

Nyoman had given him the name and location of his boss, but that didn't mean that he would be there. Legowo had said that they knew of the leader of the local Laskar Bali group, but that Aryanto had been keeping a very low profile in recent times, and hadn't been high on the POLRI persons of interest list. Kryton was starting to wonder if POLRI were using this raid as an excuse to settle some scores with the local gang.

He looked out of the window as a scooter went hurtling past; its driver obviously well adept in navigating the narrow streets and lanes of the local neighbourhood. It was now the middle of the day, and most of the residents would be at work manning the restaurants, cafés, shops, and businesses typically located further south and closer to the beaches.

How are these guys linked to the Caucasian man? wondered Kryton.

The Greyfin support team in Australia were busy working on the intelligence gained so far, especially the imagery taken by the RFSU patrol. Unfortunately, so far none of the systems or databases in the five-eyes community had been able to produce any further fidelity.

Which is why Kryton needed to speak to Aryanto. He was the only known link in the chain that hadn't been followed up.

He pulled his phone from his pocket and tapped on the buttons.

About to enter the house, he texted to Cav's phone.

A few moments later, the reply vibrated in Kryton's hand.

Ack.

A scooter pulled up alongside the Toyota, and the pillion passenger quickly disembarked. Kryton placed his hand over his concealed pistol, ready to respond to any unwanted intruder. He didn't need to worry, though, as Legowo, now wearing civilian attire, opened the door and resumed his seat behind the wheel.

"Good?" asked Kryton.

Legowo looked at Kryton and presented his trademark smile.

"We are good," he replied cheerfully.

Kryton couldn't help but smile.

It's probably not every day he gets out of the office, he thought to himself.

Legowo spoke into his radio, giving last-minute instructions to the raiding team pre-positioned in locations nearby.

Kryton looked over at the police officer. He had grown to like and respect the man in the short time they had spent together. The efficiency with which he had organised the mission, and the professional manner in which he had delivered the operational brief, was as good as any western commander Kryton had ever worked with.

The quick turnaround from mission inception to launch reminded Kryton of the time he spent as part of the Tactical Assault Group when attached to the 2nd Commando Regiment back in Sydney many years earlier, where short planning cycles were supported by well-developed tactics and intensely practised techniques and procedures.

The question now: how good were the men under Legowo's command?

And would Anyanto even be there?

The two men sat in silence for about a minute, until the final radio call came in to Legowo.

"Ready," came the final transmission in Bahasa.

Legowo looked at Kryton.

"I'll call you forward once we secure the building," he said.

Kryton nodded.

"Good luck, sir," he said sincerely.

It had been agreed that Kryton would not participate directly in the raid. It was still a POLRI mission after all, even if it was on behalf of the AFP – on their behalf as far as the Indonesians were concerned, anyway.

It would be way too overt and public, and the use of lethal force against a foreign citizen that wasn't on any kill/capture list wasn't within his remit.

The building was at the end of a T-junction, and had three avenues of ingress at the front, and a pedestrian exit at the back. Legowo had planned the mission well, and there would be no escaping for the inhabitants of the hideout.

Legowo reached into the back seat, pulled a zippered black jacket from his go-bag, and placed it on. The words *POLRI* were emblazoned in large yellow font across the back. He placed a baseball hat on his head, which was adorned with what was known as scrambled egg – the yellow braiding across the hat's visor that was commensurate to his rank.

The Indonesian took a deep breath, then pressed the button of his radio.

"Go, go, go," he said calmly in Bahasa.

Suddenly, the relative quietness of the small street was shattered as sirens and the distinct sound of screaming engines rapidly approached the compound from multiple directions.

A POLRI Ford Ranger raced to the front of the gated compound, where two officers, wearing body armour and helmets over their uniforms, tied a chain around the gate, whilst another Ford Ranger full of officers pulled up adjacent to the compound wall, where a slew of POLRI officers jumped off and took up positions, ready to make entry with their Steyr rifles. A third Ford Ranger, sirens blaring, raced past Kryton's car, spilling its cargo of POLRI officers out, all preparing to support the initial raiding team.

Legowo waited until they had driven past, and then proceeded to get out of the car and start walking up towards the front gate, which had just been violently ripped off of its hinges as the first Ford Ranger raced away.

The first team made entry, throwing flashbangs along the ground as they went.

This caused every bird in the direct vicinity to hurriedly fly away like an animal possessed, whilst the neighbourhood dogs started barking and whimpering like it was midnight on new year's eve.

Kryton smiled.

He thought about what those brave officers were feeling at that exact moment.

The excitement. The adrenalin.

He thought for a moment about his days in Afghanistan as a younger soldier, where smashing through doors to face god knows what was part of the daily routine.

What was I thinking? he thought to himself, shaking his head.

Some of the local homeowners started coming out of their residences, curious as to what all the commotion was about.

Shouting and yelling filled the street, along with the sounds of the last of the flashbangs.

Bang – bang – bang.

The sudden sound of gunfire startled some of the curious homeowners, most of whom fled back into their houses. It startled Kryton, too.

Bang – bang – bang.

Pow – pow – pow, came the reply.

"Shit," murmured Kryton, sitting a little more upright in the seat.

They were the distinct sounds of two different types of assault rifles being fired. Kryton knew them well, having spent years handling Steyrs in the conventional army, and fighting against those who would wish him dead whilst using their own AK-47s.

Several more shots rang out, indicating an unfolding gun battle.

The support team attempted to make entry at the front, only to be obstructed by the initial raiding team who were struggling to maintain their momentum in the face of what was at least one assault rifle, but from the sounds of it possibly more.

While the compound's design was suited to preventing the inhabitants from escaping, it also meant it was much easier to defend, even with a minimal number of small arms.

Kryton was about to get out of the car when suddenly a large explosion ripped through the air.

The sound was earth-shattering, to the point Kryton thought that his eardrums might have burst. He ducked down in his seat, half expecting the blast wave to shatter the windscreen.

It didn't, so he sat up in time to see a large, black plume of smoke ascending into the sky. The blast had ripped away most of the front of the compound, and flames lapped the street's electricity cables.

They must have fucking wired the place, thought Kryton.

He jumped out of the car and ran towards the unfolding drama. He watched as several POLRI officers stumbled out of the compound, carried by their comrades, with their uniforms ripped from their bodies and blood pouring from various injuries.

The gunfire had ceased, only to be replaced by the sounds of screaming and shouting. Local homeowners prevented Kryton from smoothly approaching what was left of the front, as they fled in terror in the opposite direction.

He managed to reach the front of the compound, and looked in to see a horrific scene. Several bodies lay strewn on the ground, being attended to by uninjured POLRI officers.

"Fuck me," mouthed Kryton, as he looked over to see Legowo standing in the corner, issuing orders and shouting into his radio.

Kryton ran over to him and crouched down.

"My medical kit is in the back of the car," Legowo said authoritatively.

"I'm on it," said Kryton, as he turned around to race back out of the mostly demolished compound.

He had to swerve to avoid several brave civilians who had rushed in to offer assistance to the injured POLRI officers – a vast cry from what had been briefed as a hostile part of town. The sound of sirens echoed in the distance, suggesting that Legowo had been able to call for support.

I hope they're ambulances, Kryton thought to himself as he ran towards the car.

He hurriedly opened the rear door and reached in, brushing Legowo's go-bag and some other boxes off of the back seat.

Nothing.

He paused for a moment, thinking.

"The boot!" he exclaimed to no one in particular.

He reached over to the front side and pushed on the button near the driver's console that released the boot of the car.

An audible click indicated that it had released its latch, and Kryton jumped out of the car and reefed the boot open.

He reached inside, grabbing the suitcase-sized red bag clearly marked by a green cross synonymous with first aid bags, and pulled it out quickly. He started running back up the street. The wind was channelling the thick smoke horizontally across the front of the houses, making visibility difficult.

Several more police cars were starting to arrive at the scene, making it difficult to move up the narrow confines of the street, forcing Kryton to weave in and out through the drains.

He accidentally bumped into a man wearing a POLRI shirt, ever so briefly making eye contact, before continuing his way back into the compound. It was chaos. The raiding team tried to recover their injured companions, whilst other well-meaning civilians and newly arrived officers clamoured over each other trying to help out.

Kryton ran over to a POLRI officer who was kneeling over one of his injured colleagues, trying to deal with what appeared to be a leg wound. He kneeled down and placed the first aid kit next to the officer, opening it up and rifling through it, looking for a bandage to help the injured officer attend to a deep laceration on his face.

Kryton froze.

"The scar," he muttered.

He thought back to a few moments ago, and to the POLRI officer he had momentarily bumped into. In all of the commotion, it had not even registered that the man had a scar across his left cheek.

"Here, hold this on it," said Kryton in Bahasa, taking the man's hand and placing it on the bandage now covering the side of his face.

The Australian jumped up, running to the front of the compound. He stopped and looked down the street, squinting in an attempt to see through the smoke.

About sixty metres away, he could make out a figure wearing a POLRI shirt walking away on the side of the street. Odd considering that all of the other officers were running *to* the scene. Kryton shifted his eyes slightly, looking at the bottom half of the figure.

He could see the person wearing knee-length shorts and what looked like boat shoes. Hardly the standard-issue uniform of any of the world's police units.

Kryton started moving after the man, manoeuvring through the street now cluttered with ambulances, police cars, as well as people either helping out or gawking at the terrible scenes in front of them.

He moved quickly, not being able to do anything more than a quick jog due to all of the obstacles. His height and build ensured that he was able to easily brush people out of the way, and he slowly gave chase to the man.

Kryton reached into his pocket and pulled out his phone, keeping one eye on the keys as he dialled, and the other on his suspect.

Cav answered almost immediately.

"What the fuck is going on? We just heard it on the radio," said Cav.

"It's gone to shit here, mate. They had explosives or something, and the raid must have set it off."

"Jesus," replied Cav.

"Get your escort and get over here to help out. They'll need a medic with your skills. I think I've found Aryanto. The little shit tried to sneak out. I'm following him now. Tell Legowo I'm following a suspect."

"Roger, on my way," said Cav.

Kryton ended the call and returned the phone to his pocket. He placed his hand over his concealed pistol, just to reassure himself it was still there. He steeled his eyes onto his target. The street opened up as they moved away from the carnage, allowing him to start running towards the man.

A motorised scooter suddenly came out of a narrow lane, almost knocking Kryton over, forcing him back onto his heels, and bleeding his momentum.

"Fuck sake," Kryton said loudly.

The male rider ignored him, and raced up the street, stopping for a moment next to the man Kryton was chasing.

The man went to get on the scooter.

"Hey," screamed Kryton, now sprinting up towards the two men.

He was now only thirty metres away.

The shout caused the man to look back down the road at Kryton.

There was no mistaking who it was – Anyanto.

63

10

Kryton was close enough that he could see the surprised look on Aryanto's face. The Indonesian probably didn't expect that wearing a stolen POLRI shirt over shorts and casual shoes would be a perennial disguise, but he had no doubt hoped the ruse would last longer than less than a block as he cowardly sauntered away from the compound.

Aryanto jumped onto the scooter and slapped his colleague on the shoulder. The two men accelerated away, just as Kryton lunged at the rear of the scooter. The Australian missed by mere millimetres, falling onto the dusty road.

Kryton looked up, watching as the scooter tore up the street, nearly knocking over some small children. He jumped to his feet, angry at himself for not catching up to them, and now with a furious motivation to capture the gang leader.

He sprinted again, perhaps hoping that the traffic and crowd might slow the pair down and allow him to catch up.

It didn't.

The scooter came to the end of the road and turned right, weaving its way in between the ambulances and police cars that were working their way to the scene of carnage back at the compound.

Kryton continued running, but the gap between himself and the scooter quickly widened.

C'mon, he willed himself, but beginning to realise that the effort was becoming futile.

He reached the end of the street, looking to the north and observing the scooter race away up a wider road than the street they had just come out of.

Kryton stopped in the middle of the road.

"Fuck," he said loudly, watching the gangster thugs make their escape.

A screeching of tyres shook Kryton out of his anger. He turned around quickly and saw a large metallic wall staring right at him. An additional bolt of adrenalin ran through him. For a fleeting moment, he thought that he was done for.

That was close.

He took a step back, seeing the white Mitsubishi flatbed truck that had almost cleaned him up.

The small Balinese driver looked down. His eyes looked like dinner plates, wondering how he hadn't hit the rogue pedestrian. Kryton looked back up at him, concurring with his thoughts.

He turned his head, rapidly thinking.

The best lead they currently had was quickly getting away on a scooter. Action needed to be taken.

And quickly.

Kryton raced around to the driver's side, ripping open the door.

"Get out, NOW," he said firmly to the confused driver.

The young man instinctively launched himself in the other direction, jumping over the passenger's seat and exiting the truck through the other door.

"That'll work," muttered Kryton, as he jumped up and into the driver's seat.

He closed the door and grasped the steering wheel. The elevated height afforded him a good view up the road, and he quickly regained sight of the scooter, now about ninety metres up ahead of him.

He engaged the gears. The sound of metal rubbing over metal pierced Kryton's eardrums, suggesting that he hadn't engaged the clutch far enough.

He smashed the pedal to the firewall, which resulted in a smoother engagement of the clutch, finally putting the truck into motion.

Kryton slowly gained speed, looking to his left to see the passenger door flapping against the truck's frame, the result of the driver's hasty exit.

Kryton floored the accelerator of the truck – a monster compared to the scooters and bicycles hogging the road – and further engaged the gears to increase speed. He briefly moved the wheel to the left, and then reefed on it to the right, allowing gravity and physics to do its part and forcing the passenger door to slam shut.

He focused up the road, and noticed that the gap between his commandeered truck and the escape scooter was starting to close.

However, although the speed of the truck was on his side, the size of it wasn't. Kryton slammed down on the horn on the steering wheel as he raced up the road, forcing the myriad of traffic to veer out of his way. He swerved to avoid a cart vendor who was mindlessly crossing the road, but that caused him to smash against the large leaves of an overhanging Banana Tree.

The collision ripped the side window off of its hinges, spilling glass across the road. Kryton manoeuvred the truck back onto the main part of the road. He watched as the approaching scooters and small cars violently swerved to avoid the oncoming beast, some of them being forced into the gutters or into the trees and gardens at the front of some of the houses that ran parallel to the road.

Some drivers got so close that Kryton was certain he could see the whites of their eyes. He continued honking on the truck's horn, pleading for the innocent bystanders to get out of the way.

The last thing he wanted was to cause the death of a poor old market vendor or school kid. That's pretty untidy when undertaking a covert mission, and not to mention the diplomatic incident it would cause.

But Kryton needed Aryanto. He possibly held the key to something far greater, and it was worth taking some big risks to find it.

The pair on the scooter kept racing along the road, recklessly endangering the lives of the local inhabitants in order to make their escape.

Aryanto looked over his shoulder and could see the truck starting to close in. He shouted at his companion.

"Go left," he said in Bahasa.

The driver did as he was told, leaning into the turn and going up a narrow alley. Kryton shifted gears rapidly, trying to reduce speed in order to take the turn. He pulled hard on the wheel, and for a moment he was worried the truck might flip as it leaned violently and made the ninety-degree turn within the space of a few metres.

Several boxes on the rear spilt onto the street – free merchandise for the locals who were wondering what the hell was occurring in their neighbourhood.

The Australian pulled tightly on the steering wheel, expertly manipulating the pedals and righting the heavy truck into the narrow lane.

Kryton took in a deep breath. He once again smashed down on the horn, alerting people to the danger that was now among them. The chase continued as Aryanto and his companion consistently attempted to change direction in order to lose their pursuer, only to find each time that Kryton had managed to find a way through the assortment of pedestrians, street vendors, traffic, and random obstacles that obscured the roads.

In any other place and time, the local police would have been all over such a dangerous activity occurring in broad daylight in the middle of a busy urban area. But POLRI had other matters on its mind at the moment.

Kryton drew even closer, and was now within twenty metres of the escaping gangsters. This forced Aryanto to take even bigger risks, and he instructed his companion to go onto the narrow footpath, forcing the pedestrians to dive out of the way.

Kryton remained on the road, keeping one eye firmly on the men, and the other on the road where the traffic was once again becoming denser.

They sped past the Kuta bombing monument – a shrine to the victims of the 2002 massacre carried out by the radicals of Jemaah Islamiyah, an al-Qaeda offshoot that once ran amok across the Indonesian archipelago.

Within another five minutes, the chase reached the shoreline in the western part of Denpasar, where tourists and locals alike mingled on the beachfront, continuing their daily routines or settling in for an afternoon of cocktails and seafood. Grey clouds were starting to roll in, as the usual afternoon storm started to approach.

Kryton was now close enough to the scooter that he was able to bump the rear of it, causing it to wobble and jolting to bodies of the two men on it.

Aryanto pointed to the footpath in front of a local hotel, and his companion responded by manoeuvring their scooter onto it. Kryton kept driving on the road, and remained alongside the scooter as it tore up the footpath, forcing even more terrified pedestrians to jump into the shopfronts or bushes in order to avoid being run over.

The scooter continued for another 100 metres south along the footpath, giving no regard to the safety of the people walking unassumingly along it. Kryton continued alongside them, hoping for an opportunity, and enough space, to veer into their path, hopefully knocking them off.

The two men soon drove directly into the oncoming path of several stocky tourists, who were walking in a staggered gaggle, obviously having started their pub crawl several hours earlier.

Possibly members of an Australian rugby club on their end of season trip.

Most of the inebriated men shuffled out of the way as the scooter drove past them, but one of the large men took umbrage to being forced off of his line and, perhaps thinking he was facing a front-rower, decided to tackle the mechanical opponent.

The two much smaller men came flying off of the scooter, falling into a heap among the bushes of a well-manicured garden of a luxury hotel. The scooter spun around on its axis before conducting a complete somersault, crashing into the gutter and spilling fuel from its cracked tank.

"Shit," spluttered Kryton, as he slammed both feet into the pedal of the brakes of the truck, bringing the heavy vehicle to a screeching halt and causing it to fishtail slightly.

Due to his speed, he had stopped about two dozen metres past where the scooter had been suddenly brought down. He opened the driver's side door and jumped down, weaving his way back towards the crash site in front of the hotel. Several small cars honked their horns, annoyed by the truck that was now blocking the road.

Aryanto jumped up, having been relatively unhurt in the crash. His partner had not been so lucky, and lay prostrate against a wall with a deep laceration against his head. Two of the tourists, to that point thinking the entire event had been a laugh, suddenly sobered up and reached down to try to assist him.

Another tried to help Aryanto as he stumbled away, but the Indonesian slapped away the offers of assistance. Kryton jumped over a garden bed and landed on the footpath. Aryanto saw the Australian coming after him, and started running in the opposite direction. Kryton weaved his way around the group of his countrymen, briefly looking down at Aryanto's offsider.

He didn't look good, and had obviously taken the brunt of the tackle; although his unprotected head meeting the concrete footpath had probably not helped much.

Kryton chased Aryanto on foot, racing along the footpath. They moved north, running past the collection of beachfront buildings that included a mix of modern hotels nestled in amongst the small shanty markets constructed predominantly from wood and corrugated iron.

Aryanto quickly changed direction, rapidly moving into a lane that led to a hidden market. He jumped a small fence, quickly pursued by Kryton, who was surprised by the pace of his opponent; remarkable for someone who had just come crashing off of a scooter.

The gang leader ran through the market, knocking items off of the vendors' tables and pushing people out of the way in a vain attempt to slow Kryton down. Some people screamed as their shopping day was interrupted by the chase.

Aryanto jumped over a bench, knocking into a female tourist who fell awkwardly onto the ground. Kryton followed, but his size made it difficult to navigate through the heavy foot traffic of the market.

The Indonesian made it to the other end of the market and was now almost on the road. An oblivious local vendor wheeled his cart into the exit of the marketplace, obstructing his egress. This was enough for Kryton to close the gap, and the Australian launched himself at Aryanto in an attempt to tackle him. The momentum caused the two men to tumble over a small brick wall, but not before they knocked the contents of the cart onto the street.

The fall caused Kryton to lose his grip of his opponent, and he fell into the gutter. Aryanto quickly rose to his feet and used his relative advantage to make an attempt to kick Kryton. The Australian shifted himself into a kneeling position and easily parried the poorly aimed strike. His own attempt to counterstrike was thwarted by his lack of balance, and his flailing arm was unable to make contact as Aryanto took a step backwards.

The Indonesian quickly decided that a direct confrontation was not in his best interests, and he turned and continued to run up the lane at the back of the market.

Kryton regained his balance and quickly got to his feet, continuing the chase up the lane.

Aryanto sprinted away, but Kryton could see that he was starting to struggle – the crash and subsequent fall was starting to catch up with him. The gangster crossed the lane, narrowly avoiding a pair of tourists joyriding on their own scooters. He looked over his shoulder and could see that Kryton was rapidly closing in on him.

The Indonesian was getting desperate.

He ran into a sporting goods store, knocking over a basket containing rattan kali sticks as he entered. He quickly grabbed two of them and continued running through the store, escaping out via the back door. Moments later, Kryton entered through the front door of the store. He stopped and looked around, but couldn't see his prey.

He made eye contact with the owner, who was standing behind the counter, a confused look on his face. The owner pointed to the back of the store, perhaps hoping that the intimidating Australian would catch the man who had just stolen from him and knocked over the display stands.

Kryton ran through the store and eventually entered the storeroom at the back. He noticed the rear door swinging on its hinges, so he ran over and peered through just before the door completely shut. He observed Aryanto entering what looked to be a warehouse diagonally across from the sporting goods store, still carrying the kali sticks.

Kryton gently kicked the door open, and walked into what appeared to be a cul-de-sac surrounded by industrial storage buildings. He knew that Aryanto had grabbed the sticks in anticipation of having to fight his way out of trouble, as his injuries were making a continued foot chase untenable.

He ran over to the entry of the warehouse, slowing down to a brisk walk as he neared the narrow doorway. He removed his pistol from its holster, leaving the safety on. Its purpose now would be to bluff Aryanto into surrendering. He still needed him alive.

Kryton moved across the front of the doorway, ensuring that he checked the entire arc before entering, just in case Aryanto was waiting in ambush.

He took a deep breath, trying to slow his heart rate which was elevated from the chase.

He slowly made entry.

11

Kryton paused for a moment to allow his eyes to adjust to the dimly lit cavernous warehouse. It was about the size of four basketball courts and was two stories high. Kryton slowly looked around, seeking his target.

He could see that it contained numerous small cars, neatly arranged in a manner that suggested it was a pre-sale storage facility. He noticed that the main roller door was locked and that there was no daylight shining in, apart from the small windows near the roof, that would suggest an open exit at the other side.

He unlatched the small retaining pin that held the door open and closed it behind him. He saw a small table next to the wall, and with minimal effort, he jammed it up against the door.

The two men were now locked inside. For the first time since he had identified Aryanto at the compound, Kryton felt that *he* now had the initiative.

Kryton walked along the front of the warehouse; his eyes slowly and deliberately scanning across the top of the cars, seeking the location of Aryanto. The cars were formed-up in lines of two from the front to the back of the warehouse, with an improvised walkway in between them.

He reached the side of the warehouse, observing dusty workbenches with oil barrels placed underneath them. Kryton squatted down, tilting his head and looking across along the ground and the seemingly endless rows of tyres, hoping to see a pair of feet hiding amongst the cars.

A light metallic clang suddenly disrupted the eerie silence.

Kryton jumped to his feet, moving across the side of the warehouse and attempting to get a direct view across to the source of the noise.

He decided to change tact, and started moving quickly along the rows of cars, darting in and out of the neatly arranged body of vehicles and towards the source of the noise, hoping to catch Aryanto off guard.

In about ten seconds, he had reached the opposite side of the warehouse. An open space among the cars had several wheel hubs scattered across the ground. He stood next to one of the cars, looking down at the disturbed dust that suggested that the hubs had only very recently been moved; most likely accidentally kicked and as such the likely cause of the noise.

A gentle thud sounded from directly next to Kryton's head, startling him and causing him to jump back. He quickly looked up and saw a small black and white cat sitting at the edge of the roof of the car and looking back at him curiously.

Kryton exhaled deeply, half grimacing and half smiling.

Bloody cat, he thought to himself.

The cat continued to look at Kryton, but then slightly tilted its head, now looking over the Australian's shoulder. Kryton saw a shadowy reflection in the car's side window, rapidly approaching him.

He instinctively ducked, just as a swinging rattan kali stick cracked against the window of the car, shattering the glass. The cat scattered, deciding that this wasn't his fight.

Kryton rolled towards the front of the car, adjusting his body to face his attacker from a crouched position. Aryanto stepped towards Kryton, but the Australian kicked up at the Indonesian's hip, buckling him over and forcing him backwards.

Kryton stood up, pointing his pistol at Aryanto.

"Get the fuck down…" he said, but the whipping motion of a trained kali practitioner's strike knocked the pistol out of his hand.

Kryton squatted down to try and retrieve it, but it bounced along the ground and under one of the cars. Either Aryanto had sensed that Kryton wasn't actually intending to use his gun, or he just didn't care.

Kryton quickly stood up again, as the gangster looked to press the advantage, preparing to launch a horizontal backhand strike with his second stick. Kryton adjusted his position, stepping in and turning his body as Aryanto launched his attack. This reduced the space available for the strike, and using the smaller man's momentum, he parried Aryanto violently into the side of a car.

Kryton followed up with a sharp front kick to his opponent's body, causing Aryanto's knees to buckle slightly. The operator stepped forward, grasping one of the sticks now held loosely in Aryanto's outstretched hand and pulling it from him.

Aryanto reacted quickly, ducking Kryton's own attempted strike and stepping out and away from the car.

The two men turned and were now facing each other, each firmly grasping a stick in their right hand. Aryanto was breathing heavily, and looked around to see if there was another escape option.

72

There wasn't.

They stared at each other, slowly pacing in a semi-circle as they faced off. Kryton could tell by Aryanto's slight hobbling that any attempt to run would be futile – and Aryanto knew it.

But a cornered animal is when it's at its most dangerous.

He looked at Kryton with a renewed motivation, knowing he would have to go through the Australian in order to escape.

He screamed, launching himself at Kryton with an overhead strike. Kryton blocked it forcefully; the clacking sounds of the sticks striking each other echoed across the warehouse.

The fight continued, as each man attempted or thwarted strikes and counterstrikes at a ferocious pace. Backhand. Forehand. Overhead. Uppercut. All manner of slashing and striking techniques being used in an attempt to gain the upper hand.

The violent clacking of kali sticks made it sound like an old steam engine was hurtling along the railway tracks.

They moved back and forward, and side to side; their footwork was solid, like seasoned pugilists respecting the skills of their opponent, and each trying to find a position where they could achieve the winning strike.

Both men wore some blows to the face, neck, and upper body, but nothing significant enough to cause defeat.

Aryanto swiped desperately at Kryton, who ducked easily whilst striking at Aryatno's knees. The painful blow on the nerves of the lower leg joint caused the Indonesian to cry out in agony, his already injured lower body suffering even more damage.

Aryanto took a stumbling step backwards. Kryton mirrored the movement, stepping forward and seeking another successful hit. Aryanto suddenly stopped, lowering his body and striking down onto Kryton's toes. Despite wearing durable enclosed shoes, the whipping strike was painful enough to force Kryton to flinch and force a stop to his forward momentum. He was suddenly caught off-balance, and Aryanto took the opportunity to re-direct his momentum forward and launch another strike at the head of the Australian.

Like a desperate, wounded dog, he lunged at Kryton's head, but the Australian ducked and weaved at every attempted strike. Kryton allowed the Indonesian to get closer, and as Aryanto attempted a backhand strike, he stepped in and to the side of his opponent, blocking the strike with his free hand at Aryanto's wrist, and launching a devastating blow with the butt of his own stick up under Aryanto's nose.

The blow caused the Indonesian man's head to snap back, his eyes to water, and his knees to buckle. Kryton maintained possession of the wrist, turning it outside of the man's body which put pressure on the rest of the arm, which caused Aryanto's body to turn to the outside as well. This forced the gangster down onto his back. In one swift move, Kryton pulled on Aryanto's extended arm, turning the captured wrist in the opposite direction and pivoting his own feet across the top of Aryanto's head, pulling forcefully on the arm which then forced the crumpled body onto its front.

Kryton kneeled down, manipulating the arm behind Aryanto's body and putting the wrist in a gooseneck lock.

A standard technique taught to police officers when arresting non-compliant offenders.

The defeated man struggled for a moment, but the combination of the injuries he had received, especially from the blow to the face from Kryton, meant that his ability to resist was all but gone.

Kryton maintained the wrist lock for a moment, firmly kneeling on Aryanto's back. He inhaled deeply, seeking to catch his breath. He thought about the situation, and how quickly things had all now seemingly gotten out of hand.

What had been anticipated as a routine arrest with perhaps some resistance had led to an explosion in a residential Balinese street; a chase across Denpasar in broad daylight; a crash of a scooter than had severely injured one thug, and possibly some tourists; as well as a stick fight in some dusty warehouse.

Kryton just shook his head.

Why would it be simple? he asked himself rhetorically.

He looked around. Over near the entrance he had come in earlier he could see a small office. He adjusted the positioning of his stick, placing it under Aryanto's right armpit and up behind his neck.

Kryton stood up, dragging Aryatno up with him by using the stick as a handle. In this position, a simple manipulation of his hand would put immense pressure on the nerves in the Indonesian's shoulder blade, and essentially allow Kryton to walk his prisoner wherever he wanted him to go. The fulcrum effect caused immense pain that could only be alleviated by following the motion of the simple but effective martial arts weapon.

Another technique that was often taught to law enforcement, but typically using more modern technology such as batons.

He walked Aryanto through the rows of cars and into the office, where a desk and some chairs were sitting idly. He pulled a chair out with his foot, and in one rapid motion he spun Aryanto around and pushed him down onto the chair. The light metallic chair fell back, knocking Aryanto's head into the wall before righting itself again.

Kryton found some old electrical cabling, pulling it from the wall and tying Aryanto's hands firmly behind his back.

The hapless Indonesian was struggling to breathe; his nose clearly broken and blood covering what was left of his tattered clothes. Kryton turned around and closed the door, before turning his attention back to the gangster.

The Australian paused for a moment to allow Aryanto's mind to adjust to what he could only assume was a splitting headache. He moved and stood outside of the office for a moment, pulling his phone out of his pocket and initiating a call to Cav.

"Jesus, mate. Where are you?" asked his partner over the phone.

Kryton kept an eye on Aryanto through a dirty window that looked back into the office.

"I have Aryanto," replied Kryton. "Long story, and I've made a bit of a mess chasing the little prick, too."

"Are we compromised?" asked Cav.

Kryton thought for a second, rubbing his hand across his face and removing the dirty sweat from his brow.

"No. I don't think so. I'm guessing all of the attention is back at the compound. Are you there yet?"

"Yeah," replied Cav. "Legowo is running around like a headless chook; understandably though. The Commissioner just arrived on the scene, too. There's quite a few POLRI guys hurt, some will be on their way to the ICU, but no friendly KIAs at this point."

Thank fuck, Kryton thought to himself.

As an intelligence operator, Kryton was accustomed to deliberately placing allies at risk in order to achieve hidden national strategic agendas. But having a death of an innocent person who was unconsciously being used as a pawn was a hard thing for even the most seasoned of professionals to burden.

"The blast took out an adjacent set of units. There's a few civilians that have been hurt," added Cav.

75

"And the tangos in the compound?"

"Two dead. A couple injured. So far it seems like they're no one of significance. I'm helping with the medivacs now."

"Okay," replied Kryton. "When they can't find Aryanto in there, Legowo will know that he actually was the guy you told him I was chasing."

"How do we proceed?" asked Cav.

Kryton looked back into the office. Aryanto was making funny faces and squishing up his nose, probably in an effort to make breathing easier.

"I'll send you my location. Give me ten minutes, then tell Legowo where I am. Get Watkins out there to collect us. We'll need to brief Jonas and get cover stories prepared for any media attention. I'm going to have a quick talk with this bloke and see what he knows."

"Roger," replied Cav. "Shit mate, it's a fucking disaster zone here. I hope this was all worth it."

Kryton ran his tongue on the inside of his lips and spat some bloody mucus on the ground – the result of one of Aryanto's more successful strikes.

"Me too, mate. Me too."

Kryton terminated the call and pinged his GPS location to Cav's phone. He walked back into the office. Aryanto was making some strange grunting noises, possibly still trying to act like the tough gangster. Kyton was having none of it.

He twirled the stick twice with his wrist like a rockstar drummer, before tapping it several times on the desk – an intimidation tactic often used by interrogators that usually made detainees start assuming that all sorts of the terrible things were about to happen to them.

"Look up," said Kryton firmly in English.

He knew that the Indonesian spoke English. It had said so on the file he had viewed earlier at the police station.

Aryanto slowly raised his head, then looked down to the ground again.

"The police are going to be here in about fifteen minutes," he said, leaning in and using the kali stick to force the injured man's chin up. "How many more injuries you get between now and then is entirely up to you."

12

The SUV raced into the small compound that made up the Australian diplomatic mission in Bali. The vehicle reversed into an obscure bay near the rear of the establishment, which apart from the several antennas and the small satellite dish sitting on the roof, could have easily been mistaken for any other residential location nestled in the inner part of Denpasar.

Kryton and Cav jumped out, now focusing on the actions they would need to take after the day's activities. To say that it had been an eventful day would have been a massive understatement.

A suited man called over at them from an L-shaped walkway, waving them over to the secured communications room. The two operators started walking over.

"Shit. You go on, I've got to get the notebook from the car," said Kryton, quickly changing direction and running back towards the SUV.

He opened the front passenger door, reaching into the centre console and extracting a flimsy black A5 notebook, along with the wallet he had taken out of his back pocket when he had sat down in the vehicle ten minutes earlier.

He was about to step out when suddenly he realised someone was still sitting in the front driver's seat, their hands shaking and eyes wide open, looking straight out through the windscreen.

It was Watkins.

For a very short moment, Kryton was confused at her demeanour, until it dawned on him. He placed his foot on the running board and pulled himself up onto the seat next to her.

"Never seen anything like that before?" he asked sympathetically.

She just shook her head softly, the dryness in her mouth preventing her from providing any audible response.

He looked at her and noticed some blood on the side of her blouse.

Cav had called her into the compound to RV with him and wait for Kryton to return to the scene. He had then had her assist the medics to evacuate the wounded. What was a routine activity for Cav had shocked the hell out of the young girl, who had never experienced such an horrific sight.

Kryton placed his hand on her wrist, in a small attempt to help comfort her.

"You did well out there. You helped save lives today," he said.

He looked down at the cup holder under the dashboard, and picked up a bottle of water, uncapping it and handing it to her.

"Here, drink some of this," he said kindly.

She grasped the bottle gingerly, her hand still shaking as she placed it to her mouth, taking several small sips.

Kryton could see some of the colour returning to her face. She exhaled deeply, slowly coming back into the present. Confident that she would be okay, Kryton started to get out of the SUV.

He paused when she spoke softly.

"What happened out there?" she said turning her head to look at him. "Who are you guys?"

He looked over to the communications room where Cav was waiting for him, before looking back at her. He glanced down at the wallet in his hand that was sitting on the notebook. He flicked it open, looking up and showing her the badge.

"We're the cops!?" he said humorously, trying to make her laugh.

She gave him a curious, almost knowing smile.

He smiled back at her and winked reassuringly, then closed the door and walked over to join Cav and the other man, just as the skies opened up and cooled the humid air down with a refreshing downpour.

The three men walked over to a small table, where a portable secure communications system – otherwise known as ilobs – was set up. A video connection was attached to a television screen.

"I'm Dave Wilson. I'm deputy head of station," said the suited man reaching his hand out to greet Kryton.

Kryton smiled and returned the greeting, sitting down and removing his concealed pistol and its holster from his belt and placing it on the table. After he had tied Aryanto up and arranged for Cav to get POLRI to come and detain him, he had recovered his pistol from the dusty and oil-stained ground under one of the cars in the warehouse.

He had then spent about fifteen minutes having a very robust conversation with the gang leader. By the time POLRI had arrived, Aryanto was more than happy to be taken into local custody.

"All good out there?" asked Cav motioning to the SUV.

"What? Oh, yeah. The girl was a bit shaken up. You might want to check on her later," he said whilst looking over at Wilson.

The ASIS officer nodded, loosening his necktie and taking off his jacket.

"Apologies that I couldn't be here to greet you earlier. I was stuck in Jakarta briefing the ambassador," he said.

"No worries. All good?" asked Kryton.

"Yes," replied Wilson, pulling a keyboard closer to his chair and tapping on some of the keys. "The head of station is in Bangkok this week so I had to step up in her place. Looks like I missed all of the action back here."

"I'm sorry about that," said Kryton, "and I understand we've created a bit of a mess that DFAT is now going to have to clean up."

Wilson raised his hand in a gesture that signified he didn't consider it a big problem.

"We get an average of two to three Aussie tourists a week doing something here that almost causes an international incident. Your efforts today probably aren't even in the top ten. Besides, I've done this long enough to understand how it works," said the ASIS officer, knowing that intelligence was always based on the principle of 'need to know'.

"Okay. We've been instructed by Canberra to provide every assistance to you. Your operation must be heavily compartmented, they weren't prepared to go into great detail, even with me, but they have given me the salient points, so I think I'm up to speed enough to assist," he added.

He had at very least been briefed into some of the details surrounding the assassination of Volkov at the remote mine in Western Australia; enough to support the Greyfin team, but only to the point of being able to be in a position to help them when needed. As far as he knew, it was a routine ASIS intelligence operation investigating a murder with intelligence ramifications; perhaps with a military component embedded seeing as the two men sitting next to him looked more like soldiers than regular case officers. He was smart enough to know that there was likely more depth to it, but the actual mission intent wasn't important to him – he knew that not knowing everything was part of the job.

The leaked list. A targeted assassination. The Caucasian man. All that detail still needed to be protected. The fewer people involved reduced any chances of compromise of the operation.

"No worries. Just glad that you're here now," said Kryton, understanding that their visit to Bali had been at very short notice, and that the spies in the embassy in Jakarta had their schedules organised weeks ahead.

Kryton was thankful that the locally based spy was willing to assist them without feeling undermined by a lack of information as to the true nature of the mission. He and Cav would make every effort to maintain a good relationship with the DFAT and ASIS staff whilst in-country. After all, their support was invaluable. He had seen some special forces operators treat their intelligence and diplomatic counterparts terribly in various operations over the years, and relationships between the military and other government agencies had been damaged as a result.

He knew that the diplomats would now have to smooth over what was likely to be a some very concerned and pissed off hosts within the senior ranks of POLRI and the Indonesian government; especially seeing as half of Denpasar had been blown up or placed at great risk thanks to a dangerous scooter and truck chase in the past few hours.

He appreciated that diplomacy was not all cocktail parties and visits to strip joints with corrupt host nation officials. Most of it was tedious and unrewarding work, all in the name of the national interest. He admired them for doing it.

"Our AFP LO, as in the real AFP LO, will be back here in a few hours. He'll take up the guise of this being an AFP led inquiry into the murder in WA," said Wilson.

He rubbed his eyes and looked up to the television screen, trying to facilitate a connection back to Australia. It certainly looked like he had had a very long day.

"The narrative at the moment is that POLRI conducted a raid on a gang hideout. Their publicised reason for the op is a routine operation to weed out drug runners and smugglers. Actually, the gunfight and explosions support that narrative. Laskar Bali has a history of reacting violently to police incursions into their territory," briefed Wilson.

"And us?" asked Cav, knowing that the Greyfin involvement might come under scrutiny.

"Shouldn't be an issue", replied Wilson. "Plenty of Aussies floating around Bali, wearing all sorts of clothing. A white bloke driving like a lunatic around town, even in a truck, actually happens more often than you'd think. And the AFP guys are regularly doing operations and training with POLRI, so your cover is intact."

"I checked the warehouse before I talked with the gang bloke. No CCTV," added Kryton.

"Roger that," said Cav.

Wilson kept tapping at the computer and fiddling with the cables leading to the ilobs.

"Bloody afternoon rain can be a pain in the arse for comms," he said, becoming more frustrated with the failing technology.

Kryton and Cav took a few moments to rehydrate by putting away a bottle of water each, and then started looking through the notebook.

Cav had been successful in convincing a young POLRI officer, who was part of the site exploitation team, to hand it over to him after he had found it in the rubble.

They flicked through the pages. It contained a range of columns and charts, as well as names and addresses, mostly written in Bahasa, but some of it in English.

"What do you think?" asked Cav.

"I think it's an accounts book," suggested Kryton. "Legowo said that the compound blew because the firefight ignited some unstable chemical precursors."

"So, it was a drug lab?"

"Pretty much. Legowo told me that they have raided the place before, probably about six months ago, but it was empty then. This must be a recent set-up, and they hadn't quite stabilised the production yet," said Kryton.

"Good win for POLRI, then."

The television screen flickered, and a familiar image appeared, albeit a little grainy.

It was Jonas.

"Can you blokes hear me?" he said through what was, fortunately, a very clear audio connection.

"Yeah mate, loud and clear," replied Kryton, giving the thumbs up.

"G'day Dave. How you been, mate?" said Jonas enthusiastically, suggesting they knew each other well.

"I'm buggered, mate. I spent the day in Jakarta dealing with the usual dramas. It's been a busy few days," he said, trying to stifle a yawn. "All good, though. I'm here to help your lads for as long as you need me."

"Thanks, mate, we appreciate it. I'll ask you to step out while Zach gives me a back brief," said Jonas.

"Say no more," he said happily, standing up and grabbing his own notebook and jacket. "Beers on you when I come home next month for some leave."

Jonas simply gave a thumbs up.

"I'll be in my office at the end of the walkway if you need me," he said to the two operators.

"Thanks, sir. We appreciate your help," said Kryton, ensuring that the senior ASIS officer left the room feeling the love.

Kryton and Cav adjusted their positions at the table, sitting closer to the screen. They noticed Jonas taking a deep breath.

"Okay. What the fuck is going on there?" he asked them.

"Umm...Zach?" Cav said as he looked at Kryton.

The commando then moved his seat back as he slumped down a little, turning his head as if trying to hide. He was happy for his friend to take this one.

Yeah, thanks champ, Kryton thought to himself, unimpressed.

He scratched the back of his head and composed his thoughts.

"We met up with the POLRI contact here and he briefed us on what they knew. His name is Legowo. The plane crashed on a beach near the tourist areas, and the two Indonesian blokes were caught pretty quickly."

"What about the bloke that fired at the army guys?" asked Jonas.

"He obviously legged it when they crashed. No one reported seeing him. I questioned one of the Indons that POLRI detained, and although he lied about being with the Caucasian man initially, when I showed him the photo of the plane from the beach, he still maintained that he didn't know anything about the actions at the mine site."

"We sure about that?" asked Jonas.

"Definitely. He shat himself when I threatened drug charges, but all he could tell me was the location of his boss in Denpasar. He and his brother were just lackeys who could fly a plane."

"Well, if the threat of the death penalty doesn't make them talk, then I'm not sure what else will," lamented Jonas.

"POLRI led a raid on the compound identified by my questioning. That's when it all hit the fan. They went in heavy because it was a known gang location, but it turned out they hit an active drug lab."

"What happened then?" asked Jonas, writing down his own notes.

"I located a bloke named Aryanto. He's the boss of the two locals that were on the plane. He somehow managed to escape the shitfight at their compound. He ran when I went after him."

"And that's when you turned Denpasar into Mount Panorama?" said Jonas, referring to the famous Supercars race held annually at Bathurst in regional New South Wales.

Kryton shifted awkwardly in his seat. He was mostly sure that Jonas was being sarcastical, but he felt best not to appear too nonchalant about it.

"Umm, well, yeah. I assure you no one got hurt; and, we've got deniability."

Jonas shook his head slightly, and the two operators could see him trying to hide a wry smile. They knew Jonas understood how quickly things could go sour on operations, but the fact was he would be the one having to explain to the bosses in Washington and Canberra when things started to get too noisy.

They sympathised with him.

"We have gained some good intelligence, however," said Kryton, hoping to provide some good news that would justify the intrusion into Indonesia.

Jonas looked up, interested in the details.

"I managed to get some detail out of Aryanto," said Kryton. "They frequently work with other smugglers across the archipelago, conducting various drug-running activities across the islands. Apparently, they've been running cocaine and heroin into WA for the past few months."

"Where does the Caucasian bloke fit in?" asked Jonas.

"Aryanto said that they were contacted by some people higher up the food chain, and they were instructed to fly him into WA. Legowo says that Laskar Bali is tied into numerous crime groups across the region, perhaps even some terrorist groups. Their tradecraft is old school, mostly using communications that don't involve technology – things like couriers and dead drops."

"That's not much to go off of," said Jonas.

"They get detailed to do smuggling jobs all the time, and each person only knows the person directly above him, and never knows who is higher in the chain."

"That *is* old school," said Jonas. "So, we have nothing else to go off of?"

"Hang on a sec," replied Kryton, slowly getting to the details. "We managed to get a notebook from the compound. It's got a whole bunch of information in it. I think that we can find something in it that we can use. Aryanto mentioned it to me while I was interrogating him. He said that he had been instructed to collect a man from the airport about two days before the assassination at the mine."

Jonas smiled enthusiastically. He looked above his own computer screen and waved someone over. A moment later, Jo sat down next to him.

"Hello, boys. Making trouble are we!?" she said jokingly.

Kryton just groaned and rolled his eyes.

"Hi, Jo," said Kryton and Cav simultaneously, as if they were talking to their primary school teacher.

"Let me guess," said Jonas, getting back to the details provided by Aryanto about his airport rendezvous. "A Caucasian man."

"Yes," replied Kryton. "From a flight out of Singapore. He didn't have any more details than that."

"I asked around at the site where their plane came down on the local beach. There weren't too many witnesses, but at least one or two said that they thought that possibly a third person was there," added Cav.

"He must have just been quicker at getting away than the other two he was with," suggested Jonas.

"So, you have a notebook I heard?" asked Jo.

Cav held it up to the screen.

"I'll need those pages. If you take a picture of each page and send them through, we'll conduct an exploitation and analysis on the materials inside it from here in Canberra."

"Can do," replied Kryton. "Let's see those 'unlimited resources' you promised in action, hey Jonas!"

Jonas just smiled. He knew the ball was in HQ's court now.

"Once we send the notebook details to you, we'll find a subtle way to ensure it gets back to the Indonesians, just in case the young POLRI lad Cav got it from mentioned it to his bosses," said Kryton.

"No worries," said Jo. "We'll let you know if any pages in it need to go missing."

Kryton and Cav both nodded.

"Okay, leave it with us. You two have had a long day. Dave Wilson will sort you out for the night. We'll RV again on here in 12 hours," instructed Jonas.

"Thanks, mate, we'll stand by," said Kryton, lightly tapping on the keyboard and terminating the video call.

Both men stood up, simultaneously stretching their arms out and yawning, like a cat waking from a long and comfortable nap. They both laughed.

"It has been a long day," said Cav, agreeing with Jonas' observation.

He flicked through the notebook, as if shuffling a deck of cards.

"I'll get cracking on this and send it to Jo," he said.

Kryton nodded, walking towards the door.

"I'll speak to Wilson, and see if he can't find somewhere to put us up for the night," he said.

"See if you can get us some wheels. A beer would be sweet right about now," said Cav.

Kryton shot his mate a bemused, almost insulted look, as if to say *do you even need to ask?*

Cav laughed and nodded, getting back to the task of taking pictures of the documents to send via encrypted signal back to HQ.

Kryton went to see Wilson.

I definitely need a beer, he thought to himself.

13

Kryton and Cav sat on a bench at a seafood bar overlooking the Badung Strait. The afternoon storms had dissipated, and the twilight started to settle in under a clear sky, with the sun setting in the far distance behind them.

They sat quietly and took in the view, each enjoying a refreshing Bintang beer. Kryton stared over the calm waters, deep in thought, and picked at the label with the fingernail on his thumb, slowly and mostly subconsciously removing it from the bottle whilst thinking about what had happened that day.

As performed by all military professionals, a concise after-action review ensured that any shortcomings and failings could be rectified. This allowed lessons to be learned, so future operations could benefit from the hindsight of the previous ones.

"Thinking about today?" asked Cav.

Kryton quickly returned to the present, clearing his throat, and taking a sip from his beer.

"Yeah. Just thinking about what we could have done differently," he said. "A lot of those POLRI guys got hurt today. They looked like kids, mostly."

"We couldn't know that that place would be a drug lab. Fact is, they probably would have decided to go into the hideout anyway at some point. Even if we weren't here, they still would have continued to question the two Indons from the plane, and at some point, I'm sure they would have given up Aryanto. You simply found out first," said Cav.

Kryton slowly nodded and looked at his colleague. He knew he was right. It was nice to be reassured, though.

"Besides, we've hopefully found a lead. Let's just enjoy a nice feed, and let Jonas and Jo crack into the notebook," added Cav. "We're Greyfin now. This is what we do!"

Cav raised his bottle. Kryton responded in kind, clinking it with his own.

"Absolutely. Thanks, bother," said Kryton as they toasted their efforts so far.

A young, diminutive Balinese girl walked up, carrying two plates overloaded with all types of freshly cooked seafood.

"Here you go," she said politely, a big smile across her face.

"Thanks," replied Cav, his eyes widened in culinary anticipation.

"Two more beers, please," said Kryton, looking back over his shoulder as she started to walk off.

She continued to smile and nodded in acknowledgement.

Cav wasted no time digging into the feast, diving into the plate and shoving several prawns into his mouth in one go. Kryton maintained the decorum, and started off with a freshly shucked oyster. It was only then that he realised that they hadn't eaten in quite some time.

The young waitress returned momentarily with their beers.

"Phank-woo," said Cav, talking with his mouth full, and narrowly avoiding spitting it all over her.

Kryton just looked at his mate and shook his head.

"What?" asked Cav, whilst still chewing.

Kryton took a sip of beer and returned his gaze to the water. The sky was quickly turning from a lovely shade of dark purple to the black which would signify the onset of night-time.

He looked at his watch, quickly conducting some mental arithmetic and determining that it would be a little before midnight back in Canberra.

"What's your thoughts on what we know so far?" he asked Cav.

The commando placed the fresh beer to his lips and washed down yet another mouthful of fish.

"Hard to say," he said without too much consideration. "This notebook will hopefully lead somewhere. The key is still the assassination at the mine. We need to find out who would go to all the effort to sneak into the country to do it. And more importantly, why? – I mean, why now? Why so long after the bloke had been put into hiding?"

"Well, that's what we're here to find out," said Kryton, impressed that the special forces operator was starting to think more analytically.

Greyfin hadn't been created to be just muscle. It was created to be *thinking* muscle.

"Also, we need to find out *how* they found Volkov," Kryton added.

"Someone on the inside?" suggested Cav.

Kryton shrugged his shoulders.

"No idea. But I imagine something like that is pretty compartmented. He sounded like a pretty important dude. Someone who the Russians would like to get their hands on if he had defected. If it *is* the Russians, they would have had to go to great lengths to get the intelligence related to his new identity and location."

"Fuck me," said Cav, suddenly taking on a serious tone, "those guys don't fuck around."

Kryton sighed and took a sip of his beer.

"No, mate. They don't. They're unforgiving, too. Look at what they did to that double agent of theirs hiding out in England. They poisoned him, *and* his daughter, in broad daylight. That's pretty brutal."

Both men sat silently and looked out over the ocean, pondering the potential reality of the threat they might be facing.

"Let's just enjoy these for now," said Kryton, raising his bottle. "We'll see what they find out for us in the morning."

14

Kryton kicked the end of the army style stretcher with his foot, looking down at the body slumped under a blanket. A muffled groan emanated from the head that was propped up by a crumpled shirt, which acted as an improvised pillow.

Not getting the response he was after, Kryton kicked it again, just a little harder this time.

The body turned over, grunting as it did so.

"What?" said Cav in an annoyed voice, wiping the drool from his mouth.

"Brief with Canberra in ten minutes," said Kryton, looking down at the sorry sight.

"Urghh, yeah, alright," said Cav, waving Kryton away and rolling back over.

Kryton shook his head and left Cav to sort himself out. Although they had taken the smart approach and returned to the diplomatic compound at a decent hour, Cav had decided to accept the invite of some of the DFAT staff who were hosting their American counterparts for a party.

In actuality, it was more of a self-invite – but he had gone nonetheless.

Kryton walked back to the comms hut and engaged in some general conversation with Wilson for a few minutes. The ASIS officer had just sent his daily memo off to the embassy in Jakarta, from where it would be added to the cables that all of the Australian diplomatic missions globally sent daily to Canberra.

Mostly it was just general information about happenings in-country that might be of interest to the department, with the odd classified piece of intelligence attached that might grab the attention of the minister, or perhaps even the PM himself.

89

"The connection is set up, you just need to make the link. I'll leave you to it," said Wilson.

Kryton thanked him and sat down at the table at the other end of the room. An almighty thump disturbed the relative silence, as Cav made his entry, opening the secure door with much more force than was necessary.

The noise was twice as loud for Cav, who rubbed his head as he walked over to the table to take a seat. Kryton gently pushed a cup filled with warm coffee over to his friend.

"Ahh, cheers," he said.

Cav took several sips, taking in some deep breaths before rubbing his eyes.

"Good?" asked Kryton.

"Yeah," replied Kryton, clearing his throat. "Let's do it."

Kryton chuckled as he looked his dishevelled friend up and down.

"Perhaps let me do the talking," he said as he played with the computer to establish the video connection to Canberra.

Cav sat back in his seat and nodded, taking in more of the coffee.

After a few moments, Jonas and Jo appeared on the screen.

"Morning, gentlemen," said Jonas in a firm tone. "Let's get to it."

Kryton and Cav just looked at each other. It was rare for Jonas to not even engage in a bit of small talk first. Kryton assessed that he had not slept in a while.

"What's the situation?" he asked.

"Okay, a few things," commenced Jonas. "Firstly, the exploitation of the notebook has given us a name, and we think it's of the guy we've been looking for."

"Who is he?" asked Kryton.

Jonas switched the screen so that the operators in Bali could see what he was talking about. It showed several CCTV pictures of a man, who was carrying a backpack and walking through what appeared to be airport security.

"This was taken at Changi airport last Friday morning. The details from the notebook referred to a man with the name of Andrew. It also had a flight number and origin, which was Singapore via Jakarta."

Kryton and Cav looked closely at the images. It did appear very similar to the other images of the Caucasian man they had seen previously.

"Aryanto's contact must have given him details about a pick-up time, and he collected Boyd from the airport in Denpasar," added Jo.

"Boyd?" asked Kryton, looking at one of the images of the notebook on the screen.

"Boyd is his surname. Andrew Boyd. At least, that's the name we pulled from the passport our friends at NSA have been able to elicit from Indonesian border control. It was used by the Caucasian man to enter Indonesia," said Jonas.

"Let me guess, it's fake," said Cav, doing his best to look engaged by saying as little as possible.

"It is," said Jo. "We've been able to track it back to Dubai, but we have been unable to find any record of any trips previous to then."

"Seems simple enough," said Kryton.

Jonas changed the images on the screen. An Australian passport profile appeared, showing a man obviously different to the man in the images from Changi's CCTV. Kryton looked at the name on it.

"Andrew Boyd!?" he said curiously.

"This is the actual Andrew Boyd," said Jo. "The number on the passport used to enter Indonesia is the same name as belonging to this Andrew Boyd."

"So, who is this bloke?" asked Kryton.

"Andrew Boyd – the real Andrew Boyd – went missing in Amman, Jordan, two years ago. He was working for an NGO based out of London. We assume that he's probably now dead," said Jo.

"Assumed?" asked Kryton. "Is there no way to find that out for sure?"

"The analysts are still looking," replied Jonas. "However, it's a common name, and death records are often buried deep in archives of wherever he died; that's assuming it was ever reported at all. On top of that, he's not on any missing persons list; at least, not in Australia. We're trying to look into similar lists in the UK, and with INTERPOL."

"Why wasn't it flagged in our passport system?" asked Kryton.

"Home Affairs only places alerts on passports where criminal activity is suspected or known, or for intelligence purposes," said Jonas. "Boyd didn't match either of those thresholds. The only admin issues he would have had would have been associated with overstaying his visa in Jordan, but nothing like that was ever reported to us by Jordanian law enforcement. Someone overstaying a visa is not as big an issue for them as it is for us or the Americans."

"And if no one reported that he was dead, then his passport would still have been active and in date," added Jo.

"So, this bloke we're chasing used a passport that was duplicated after being obtained off of a missing Aussie in Jordan, then used to get from Dubai to Indonesia via Singapore," recapped Kryton. "That means a state actor is likely involved?"

"Correct," said Jo. "And whilst our analysts still have the Russians as the likely suspects, it does also open up the possibility that other nations might be involved."

Cav sat up in his chair, his mind struggling to focus in his current condition – but focusing enough to follow the briefing.

"Wait one second," he said, a confused look on his face. "Why did he travel on a passport to Bali, but then sneak into Australia. I mean, why not just continue into Australia. It was one of our passports after all."

"It's just a matter of tradecraft," responded Kryton. "Using a fake passport can be risky, and they couldn't be sure that the passport hadn't been flagged by our border force for entering Australia. Besides, in undertaking an assassination, you want to ensure things can't be traced back to any single point that might provide a lead, and you need to leave as little evidence of your presence as possible; that includes any digital trails."

"Such as by using a passport to go through an airport in the same place you conducted the assassination," added Jo.

Cav nodded, getting a better understanding of the dynamics of it all.

"They made a deliberate disconnection between going through Bali, and entering and exiting Australia to conduct the assassination. Whoever's behind this are professionals," observed Kryton. "What about facial recognition from the CCTV, as well as the images the RFSU patrol managed to get. Has that produced anything?"

"We're still working on that," replied Jo. "So far, there is nothing on any of the five-eyes systems. We're now trying to access other potential sources, but that is going to take time, seeing as we're having to illicitly tap into other databases around the world."

Cav stood up and walked around the room, stretching his legs and taking it all in, and trying to stop the raging headache he was still suffering.

Kryton leaned into the table, flicking through the notebook they had obtained at the Laskar Bali compound and sent back via encryption to Canberra.

"What now?" he asked.

"Well, the good news is that NSA and ASD have been able to shut down on open source what was actually pretty minimal news traffic about the POLRI raid on the compound. Therefore, we're still confident that whoever we're chasing still believes that their op hasn't been compromised," said Jonas.

"How so?"

"Because the same passport used under Boyd's name was used to depart Indonesia this past Monday morning. If they assumed it was all compromised, then it would have been disposed of."

Kryton thought for a moment, doing the calculations in his head.

"He must have gone straight from where the plane landed on the beach to the airport for his exfil," he said.

"It looks that way. We suspect he flew back to Jakarta, then out via the international airport. It was well planned, but he must have been cutting it fine to get his flight, seeing as they were delayed in Australia," said Jo.

"But if he flew out of Bali before the raid on the compound, what's to say that he hasn't since disposed of it, by assuming even the smallest risk of compromise. I mean, he did shoot up the diggers on the beach; wouldn't that have been enough to make them think it had gone tits up and to change their plans?" said Cav.

Kryton looked at his colleague and smiled.

"Good point," he whispered.

"Well, if I was in his shoes, I'd be confident that making the trip into and out of WA via the drug smuggling plane would be enough to ensure that there was no trail back to the fake passport. We have an indication to support this theory," said Jo.

Kryton smiled. He knew Jo, and her analytical abilities, well enough to know that she was sitting on something.

"You know where he is, don't you!" he said.

Jo smiled back, tilting her head slightly with a touch of self-confidence.

"Well, we *think* we do," she said, trying to remain humble. "Once we determined that the passport had originated in Dubai, we started chasing it back to that location."

"And?" said Kryton.

"And we got a hit," she replied enthusiastically. "The passport was used as identification to check in to the Tamani Hotel in Dubai last night. We then placed a BOLO for the passport, and the name Andrew Boyd, through the usual channels with the Emiratis. So far, nothing matching that profile has attempted to pass through any international departure ports."

"So, he's still there?" asked Cav.

"We think so," said Jonas.

"Is there a risk the Emiratis will arrest him?" asked Kryton.

Jonas shook his head.

"Negative. The BOLO was placed with the caveat that we be alerted to his movements if the passport or the name pings on one of their systems. We didn't seek an arrest warrant with it."

Kryton and Cav leaned back and looked at each other, giving each other an approving nod. This meant that the mess that had unfolded a day earlier might actually have a silver lining.

"What now?" asked Kryton, already preparing for the next steps.

Jonas opened a folder and shuffled through some paperwork. He quickly found what he was looking for – the details of the next part of the mission.

"Okay," he commenced, a ballpoint pen hanging out of the corner of his mouth. "We're in the process of placing surveillance on Boyd in Dubai."

"Who are you putting on him?" asked Kryton.

"Considering the quick turnaround on this, we are unable to get any ASIO surveillance teams into the country. The US aren't in a position to assist, either. Fortunately, a small team of army HUMINT operators are rotating out after a deployment in Iraq. They're surveillance qualified and we've requested support from HQJOC. They will be briefed in, and will establish the operation until you get there."

Kryton smiled. It was quite likely that he had trained most of the team during his previous service. He was confident in their skills; enough for what should be a routine operation in a permissive urban environment full of westerners.

"When will they be in place?" he asked.

Jonas looked at his watch, quickly adjusting for the time difference between Australia and Dubai.

"Within the next six hours. We'll get the particulars of the team and send them to you. Their mission will be to strictly observe and make note of his movements, recording anything of intelligence value. We want to know who Boyd is, and it's likely he's got connections in Dubai who can shed some light on what is going on."

"Yep. Happy with that," said Kryton. "What are the logistics from here?"

Jo leaned forward and gave the details.

"Clay and I will take a US Air Force C-17 to Jakarta. We'll pick you two up, then it's on to AMAB," she said, referring to the Al-Minhad Air Base located in the sandy desert of the United Arab Emirates.

The Emiratis had been good enough to allow several allied nations to use a remote part of the base to house their military operations. The Australian compound was known as Camp Baird, and it acted as the headquarters for all Australian military operations in the Middle East.

Kryton and Cav knew it well. They had passed through there numerous times before moving on to the combat zones of Iraq and Afghanistan. Camp Baird was managed by the RAAF, and it contained air-conditioned huts, a well-stocked mess, as well as a café that served ice-cold drinks.

All the more reason for the soldiers of the Australian Army to resent their aviator counterparts; even if they did often overlook the fact it was manned in equal numbers by soldiers and sailors, as well as the fact that the RAAF had also had a long presence in the dangerous warzones conducting air operations that were vital to the ongoing ground missions.

Mere semantics in the long-running and friendly inter-service rivalries.

"Wilson will arrange for you to get to Jakarta. We've organised some kit for you, and you'll be able to rest and change gear in-flight," added Jonas.

Kryton looked at Cav.

"Thank goodness," he murmured, casting a judgemental eye over his hungover colleague.

Cav returned the glare, looking insulted until he placed his nose into his shirt and took a whiff.

"I might have a shower before we fly," he said sheepishly.

Kryton just shook his head.

"Okay, Jo," he said. "We'll see you in Jakarta."

15

The young USAF pilot gently entered a slight adjustment of course into the autopilot system of the C-17 as it cruised at 35,000 feet to the south of Sri Lanka. He rubbed his eyes as he looked out across the starry night. A dim red glow emanated from the control panel, just dull enough to allow him to maintain his night vision.

It had been a long mission. Commencing in Guam, they had flown to Australia, picked up the supplies needed by the embassy in Jakarta, and then flown onto the Indonesian capital. A fortnightly routine mission for the flight team. He would give his co-pilot a few more hours of rest before waking him for the final approach into AMAB.

As to the purpose of the four strangers he now had tucked amongst the cargo in the rear of the sprawling fuselage, he could only guess. His orders said to escort four VIPs to Dubai, so that is what he would do.

With luck, they would avoid some of the strong air currents typical in this region, and arrive in the early hours of local Dubai time as expected.

Kryton stood next to the plane's small kitchenette. He poured some hot water from the urn into a mug. He would let the tea bag sit for only a short while, just enough to make it a weak drink with some flavour. He grabbed the second mug and walked over to where Jo was tapping away on a laptop, seated to the side of the plane and leaning on an army-issued trunk. A small light globe provided enough white illumination to allow her to work, but otherwise the rest of the plane was in darkness, save for a few dull red lights scattered along the fuselage that allowed the loadmaster to do his routine checks.

"Have some of this," he said quietly, handing the mug of coffee to Jo.

She looked up from her screen, adjusting her eyes as she did so. It was obvious that she had been looking at the screen for quite some time.

She smiled as she stifled a yawn.

"Ah, thanks," she whispered.

Kryton sat down next to her. They sat in silence for a moment as they sipped from their respective mugs. The dull hum of the plane's engines was slightly drowned out by the intermittent snoring coming from the two special forces operators slumped across the cargo netting in the aisle of the plane. The often-hostile game of cards between the two highly competitive alpha males ended in an amicable draw hours earlier.

They both laughed.

Kryton rubbed his hand over his face. He was also tired, but he'd managed a few hours of kip in the first part of the flight. He'd always struggled to sleep on planes. He preferred a dark room and no noise.

As a soldier, though, he had learned to force himself to get rest whenever, and wherever, time and space permitted.

He leaned over closer to Jo, looking at her screen.

"So where are we at? Anything else on the not actual Boyd?"

"Afraid not," she replied disappointingly. "There's no facial recognition in any of our accessible systems, and we're now looking into wider Laskar Bali affiliations to see if any particular details come to light."

Kryton sighed deeply.

"He has to be someone," he said without conviction.

She looked at him, sharing his frustrations.

"How about the bloke murdered in the mine. What more do we know about him?" he asked her.

She leaned back into her seat, taking another sip of her coffee before speaking again.

"Around the middle of the last decade, our friends at CIA helped a group of nuclear scientists escape Russia and placed them in protection programs all over the world. Volkov was one of these scientists."

"Why? Who were they really?" asked Kryton.

"From what they would tell us, these people were highly trained specialists essentially being farmed out to help work on the nuclear programs of several rogue nations."

"What, like North Korea?" asked Kryton.

"Maybe. There are a number of countries looking to establish or improve their programs in violation of international treaties. Iran, North Korea, Pakistan, and India. Even Venezuela has been accused of attempting to develop a nuclear program."

"Jesus," muttered Kryton. "Why would the Russians do that?"

"Russian intelligence typically conducts activities that keep western agencies running around chasing information; any activity that keeps us preoccupied, and otherwise focused not on what Russia is actually doing. Anything nuclear-related is definitely going to catch our attention and focus. It forces us to have to keep an eye on many things at once."

Kryton chuckled softly. He tilted his head to look at Jo.

"The whole secret lies in confusing the enemy, so that he cannot fathom our real intent – Sun Tzu!"

She smiled and nodded in agreement.

"Well fortunately for us, Volkov managed to approach the Americans to tell them all about it. It seems the US had also got wind of this program through their deep-cover agents, and learned that the scientists were doing it against their will. The Russians denied it, of course, but there was enough evidence to suggest that an illegal sharing of knowledge was occurring. The CIA acted, and offered protection to the scientists. A new life. A new identity."

"Yeah, but in exchange for exactly what?" asked Kryton sceptically.

Jo looked at him and shrugged her shoulders.

"Ostensibly, they would share the information they had about the Russian nuclear program, as well as information about the projects they had been working on. Volkov had been asked to work for us. Jonas said he was helping conduct uranium enrichment for civilian purposes, but who really knows. Apart from that, I have no idea. Super-secret stuff!" she said. "And now, if our assessments are correct, it seems that the Russians are looking to close out the program by eliminating the scientists."

Kryton leaned back and looked at the roof of the plane, where a large US flag hung. He sat with his thoughts. This was all starting to sound like something straight from a spy book. To conduct a covert assassination in a western nation was not beyond the threshold of the Russian intelligence services. But it had never happened in Australia before.

"Do you think the scientists knew about each other's locations?" he asked Jo.

She shook her head.

"No. That would be terrible practice. Whoever is doing this obtained highly sensitive information about the new identity and location of at least one of the scientists. NSA is undertaking checks now to see if any systems were hacked in order to steal the details of more identities, as well as chasing the source of the original breach. Apparently, it was all managed by ASIS and CIA jointly, and possibly even with the British MI6. And we can't rule out the human factor, either. Has someone betrayed them from the inside?"

"What is being done to protect the others in the program?" he asked. "They'd be at risk now, too."

"Measures are being taken to ensure their safety. We have to assume they have also been compromised. Our job is to find out who Boyd is; find out how he found Volkov; who directed it; and, to find out if the others are in danger, too."

Kryton nodded his head as he played with the tea bag hanging from his mug. He pondered. The intelligence was starting to build, but there were still so many questions to be answered.

Was it Russian Mafia?

Maybe.

Was it an individual gripe?

Possible – but who had the resources to do all that had been done alone?

State-sanctioned assassination?

That was the likely scenario – but no one really wanted to think what that meant from a geopolitical point of view.

Perhaps the Russians were covering their arses. If true, they were taking some pretty big risks to do it. And why now? Why five years later? Maybe it had taken them that long to find the defectors.

So many questions.

Kryton stood up and stretched his arms out, stifling a yawn. His attention turned to the young USAF airman waving his torch over the various switch boxes internal to the aircraft, ensuring all was in working order as part of his checks.

He looked down at Jo. She looked tired. Very tired.

Even though he and Cav and been undertaking the operation in the field, he appreciated that she and the analytical team had probably slept very little over the past week since the assigning of Greyfin's inaugural mission.

"Why don't you try for some sleep?" he suggested, sitting back down next to her.

She smiled at him, appreciative of the gesture.

"Soon," she said softly. "Oh, by the way, have a look at this. This is the team in place undertaking surveillance on Boyd."

She pressed a few buttons on the laptop, bringing up six images. They were profile pictures of the army surveillance team. Kryton examined them closely.

"They look so young," he noted, not without a sense of appreciation of his own age.

"Know any of them?" she asked.

He pointed at the image of a young blonde female, stoically looking into the camera, dressed in full army ceremonial uniform and wearing the beret of the Australian Intelligence Corps.

It's what soldiers commonly referred to as the 'death photo' – its main purpose being to provide a photo for your hometown paper should you meet an unfortunate demise whilst on operational service.

"Captain Michelle Lewis," Jo read from the screen.

"I taught her at RMC. Smart girl. Very motivated, too," he said. "The others look new, though."

Jo looked at her watch.

"They've been in place for nearly 12 hours now. The latest update indicates that Boyd has turned in for the night at the hotel."

Kryton stroked his chin in thought, looking like something was concerning him.

"What is it?" asked Jo.

"Six is about the right number to watch one person. But they'll be getting tired. It would be nice to be able to rotate them soon," he said.

Jo looked at the two lifeless corpses sprawled across the cargo net nearby and snoring loudly.

"Well, we're four at least."

Kryton smiled.

"Indeed, we are. I guess we're lucky they were rotating through Dubai at the time," he said, drinking the remaining tea in the mug and placing it under his seat.

The USAF loadmaster walked past, reaching his hand out with a smile and gesturing for Kryton to hand him the mug.

"Oh, thanks mate," said Kryton, handing the young man the mug. "How long?" he asked, leaning in towards the airman and pointing to the notional watch on his wrist.

The loadie placed four fingers up towards the sky and manoeuvred the microphone on his headset away from his lips.

"Four hours," he mouthed quietly, probably because he was simultaneously receiving information from the cockpit through his headset.

Kryton gave the thumbs up, sitting back down onto his seat.

The airman nodded as he walked off to continue his duties.

"Our team in Canberra is in direct contact with the ASIS LO in the intelligence cell in AMAB. We'll get updates as it goes along," said Jo, essentially telling him to stop worrying as there was nothing they could do to help until they landed.

He nodded, showing her that he understood.

"Are you ready for this? This is the real thing now, no more training," he said to her.

She looked back at him, as if she couldn't believe that he had asked her the question.

"Don't worry. I'll keep an eye out for you," she retorted triumphantly in the style of banter they were now accustomed to with each other once again.

Kryton went to say something, but he had no words. He smiled, leaned back against the side of the plane and closed his eyes. He knew she was ready.

Within ten minutes, he was fast asleep again.

Five minutes later, so was Jo.

They would need the rest.

16

In vicinity of Tamani Hotel
Dubai metropolitan area
1130 local - Friday

Kryton wound down the window of the passenger's seat of the white Toyota Camry and tipped the remainder of the contents of a bottle of ice tea onto the dusty asphalt. What had started as a cool, refreshing beverage had quickly turned a sickly warm, and he wasn't keen on finishing it.

The humid hot air of Bali had now been replaced by the extreme dry heat of the Middle East, and he quickly returned the window to the closed position to prevent any more of the cherished cool air of the car's air-conditioner from escaping.

He turned to Captain Michelle Lewis, sitting next to him in the driver's seat who, like Kryton, was also wearing civilian clothes.

"I'll have to get used to this heat again," he said.

She looked at him and smiled.

"I think it's a bit hotter than usual today," she replied.

They both looked ahead as a taxi drove past the front of their car, which was currently hidden in plain sight in a carpark. The driver looked confused, holding his position for a moment whilst looking for his fare. He quickly gave up before driving off to seek another customer.

Over the past seven hours, the Greyfin team had arrived at AMAB, received an intelligence brief in the Camp Baird SCIF from Jonas' team in Canberra – which hadn't provided any updates of significance – and, after donning their radios and other required equipment, had joined up with the army surveillance team in place on the ground.

The ten-person team was now spread out either within or nearby the Tamani Hotel, where they had, to use an operational term, 'housed' the target for the evening. This meant that although they didn't formally have eyes on him, they had all possible avenues and exits covered.

He wouldn't be going anywhere without being seen by them.

Lewis had given Kryton an extensive brief on the situation, before handing over control of the operation to him. She was grateful to now have some support in place. Her team had been light on manpower, and they had spent the majority of their time since being assigned to the task following Boyd across central Dubai.

Kryton had conducted his assessment of the situation upon handover from Lewis, and decided it was calm enough to allow the army team to start getting some rest. Two of them were now sitting in the other Toyota Camry at another building's carpark on the other side of the Tamani Hotel, fast asleep. Jo sat in the front, monitoring the radio.

Cav and Dalton were postured inside on the ground level of the hotel, pretending to be enjoying an early lunch whilst monitoring the exits. The remainder of the army team were moving around the outside of the hotel, mingling among the pedestrians in the busy tourist area of the bustling city.

The entire surveillance team were connected by covert radios which would allow them to discreetly communicate and transmit information to each other, whilst Kryton relayed information back to Canberra via the secure satellite comms radio, where the Greyfin operations team were set up in the highly classified secured room to monitor and support the mission in real-time. Unfortunately, the op was otherwise devoid of the technical equipment they would ideally have had access to on a mission that had afforded them more planning time, such as covert cameras, CCTV hacking, and perhaps even disguises to allow them to get closer to the target.

Their mission remained to watch Boyd, and to try to see who he might be interacting with.

So far, he hadn't met with anyone or done anything of significance.

At least, to their knowledge.

Kryton had looked in detail at the profiles of the team back on the C-17 with Jo. Although he trusted their training – especially considering he had written most of the doctrine – he had also noted that most of them lacked deep operational experience.

His own team's presence among them would help identify anything that an inexperienced eye might miss.

He fiddled with his satellite radio handset, which was the size of an early 80s mobile phone

"Jonas. You receiving me?" he said into the handset.

"Loud and clear," replied Jonas, standing beside an analyst's desk and watching a large blank screen against the wall.

The words *No Signal* flickered in the middle of it.

"UAV support is still a few hours out. We're still trying to get the okay from the Emiratis to operate a Predator in their airspace. We're telling them it's a training mission," he added.

"You think they doubt that? We've been doing it for years," said Kryton.

"No. It's because we're trying to do this with no notice, and the air traffic is busier than usual today. We just have to wait our turn."

"Roger," replied Kryton.

"Guess we're doing it old school," he then said to Lewis.

The young captain nodded, yawning and rubbing her eyes.

"I've got this. Get some kip if you can," he offered her kindly.

"Thanks, but I'm okay. I'd rather that my team get some sleep first."

"Suit yourself," he said to her nonchalantly.

Nice, he then thought to himself, impressed by her leadership approach.

He looked at his watch, then around their current location in the carpark. Dubai had only recently implemented a change of routine by where the weekend days would be the more western Saturday and Sunday, as opposed to the traditional Islamic weekend of Friday. This had been done to better integrate the massive western business and tourist population of the manufactured city, which had only thirty years ago been little more than sand.

A busy urban environment had both pros and cons for conducting mobile surveillance. It was easier to hide amongst all of the people going about their daily business, but it also made it harder to keep an eye on a target who could also benefit from all of the pedestrian traffic.

Kryton pressed the button on the handset of the team radio.

"All callsigns. This is Dingo Sunray. Radio check. Over."

One by one each team member, those who were not asleep, acknowledged the call. Mobile surveillance, although appearing sexy in the movies, was in fact one of the most boring aspects of intelligence gathering. The main reason being that the word 'mobile' often ended up being replaced by the word 'static'. It was only mobile if the target was moving.

For now, it seemed like Boyd was enjoying a Friday locked up in his hotel room. Ideally, they would love to have some technical support tucked away near his room on the 15th level, which would allow them to see who was going in and out. The team had worked hard to find even that little bit of information out yesterday, but they had to be careful not to get too close with such a small team, especially if the target had counter-surveillance training, which if the intelligence assessment about his origin was correct, he likely did.

Kryton looked down at a small A5 folder, flicking through some of the notes – a log of the surveillance activity up to that point.

"Try to also track where your team is at each stage. It will help you manage their fatigue," he said to Lewis, the instructor in him always taking an opportunity to pass on his knowledge.

She looked down at the notes.

"Oh, sorry. Yep, I can do that," she said almost sheepishly.

"Oh no, it's not a criticism," he said empathetically whilst smiling. "It'll just add some polish on what has been a well-run op so far."

She nodded, clearly showing she was taking on the advice.

He had been impressed by her so far. Her handover was articulate; her concern for the welfare of her team was commendable; and, she didn't become defensive or make excuses when he gave her that little bit of advice, unlike some officers that he had trained tended to do.

He could envisage her commanding a unit one day back in Australia.

He looked back out through the windscreen.

"I don't suppose you can give us a little more info about this guy, could you?" she asked, capitalising on their friendly interactions to this point.

Kryton smiled to himself. It was HUMINT 101 – when the opportunity to ask the question presents itself, you ask it.

He also empathised with her. He knew that her team had spent the past six months diligently conducting risky operations in Iraq and the surrounding regions, and then just as they were about to go home, they get tasked to support another operation that lacked detail or context.

He understood how she felt. It's the entire reason he himself had decided to enter the mysterious world of military intelligence after having cut his teeth as a paratrooper.

Australian soldiers – indeed any soldiers – would do almost anything asked of them by their political masters. The only thing they usually wanted in return was to know why.

He hesitated for a moment, quickly recalling what he *could* tell her, and what he *should* tell her. They weren't always the same, especially in a world where the 'need to know' principle usually applied.

However, as far as he was concerned, not only was she a colleague, she was also part of his op. He could tell her whatever he wanted.

"About a week ago, a man was murdered at a remote mine site in WA. That might seem innocuous enough, but it turns out that the victim was a pretty important person."

"Who was he?" she asked curiously.

"Well, let's just say that he was the sort of person whose death caused some pretty senior people sitting in the fancy offices to want answers as to why he was killed, and caused just as many questions about who might have been involved," he said, providing enough information to quench her curiosity, but being vague enough to not divulge all of the details.

"He must have been important," she said.

Kryton opened a fresh bottle of water and took a sip, replacing the lid and placing it down in the console next to his seat.

"The person who did it, and the people working with him, tried to escape Australia on a smuggling plane. They had mechanical issues and were forced to land on some remote beach in the middle of nowhere. It just so happened that an RFSU patrol was at that exact place at that exact time."

Her eyes widened and she turned her head suddenly. The look on her face suggested that a mental itch had just been scratched.

"I heard about that from a friend at a unit in Perth. They said that there was a patrol that had been fired upon by what he said might be drug smugglers. He also said the unit had been told to keep quiet about it, too," she said, pulling a face that suggested she clearly knew someone had spoken out of term.

Kryton chuckled. The best way to ensure a secret was kept was *not* to tell people to keep it. The Australian Army was one of the biggest gossip machines going around. The same could be said for any army, really.

"Yeah, something like that. Anyway, we've been tracking the lead person involved. He's sitting up in that hotel right now," he said, motioning towards the towering hotel nearby.

Lewis exhaled deeply. Up to that point, she had only believed that her team might have been following some potential low-level spy, or at best some diplomat who was suspected of illegal activity.

He noted her comprehension of what she was now involved in. He could tell that this added an element of excitement, or at very least importance, even if it didn't change the actual mundane routine of surveillance duties.

"Sunray. This is Clay. Possible target movement in my location."

Kryton and Lewis both sat up, adjusting their positions in their seats and switching their focus to the radio call.

"Roger," replied Kryton.

Over in the hotel, Cav and Dalton remained in their seats, facing each other and finishing their lunch. Cav held a newspaper in his hand in front of him as he lounged back in his seat, just at the right height to allow him to look over the top of it and observe Boyd walking across the large hotel foyer and towards the concierge desk. He had motioned this to Clay who, facing away from the foyer, had made the call to Kryton.

"Jonas. Possible movement by target. Standby," said Kryton into the satellite radio.

"Standing by," replied Jonas, still looking at a blank screen in the ops room.

The Australian commando calmly kept an eye on Boyd with his peripheral vision, playing to his cover of a western tourist enjoying a lazy Friday with a friend in the restaurant of an expensive hotel.

Boyd spoke to a young man at the concierge desk. He signed a piece of paper, then handed a small item to the concierge, who smiled as he nodded at the large, imposing guest.

Cav pretended to scratch his mouth, whispering to Dalton. The SEAL quietly talked into his radio.

"Target has passed item to concierge," he said simply.

Kryton made a note of it in their surveillance log. If the opportunity presented itself, they might follow it up at a later point. It was probably only his room key, but any actions a surveillance target undertook needed to be noted as it might prove meaningful at a later point.

Cav watched as Boyd walked to the northern exit. The target stopped for a moment, looking over some tourist brochures at the information stand. Boyd picked up a couple, then placed them into his folded newspaper, which he tucked under his arm before walking off and outside.

"All callsigns, this is Frogman One. That's target out of the northern exit. Light blue jacket covering white polo; beige chinos; aviator sunglasses. Newspaper under his left arm," said Dalton over the radio, informing the team of the target's movements.

It was now a mobile surveillance op again.

Kryton relayed the information to Greyfin HQ.

17

The two operators sat stationary as Boyd walked into the open air. He stopped and looked up to the blue sky, taking off his glasses and cleaning them by rubbing them on his shirt.

He stood there for at least a minute, allowing his eyes to adjust to the daylight before moving off and walking around the front of the building.

Every step was being watched.

"Target heading west along Al-Sharta Road," relayed the army surveillance operator standing in the foyer of the building across the road. "Dingo Six is following now."

Kryton tracked the movements on the electronic map he had on a tablet placed on his lap. He would be able to continually track the movements of Boyd as the team sent their locations, and relay them in real-time back to Canberra.

He would be able to guide the team into a position to follow Boyd wherever he went, either by foot or by car. One team member would constantly maintain eyes on the target, supported by a second team member who could quickly take over the follow if the first member believed that they may have been spotted. It was common practice to rotate the team members through sufficiently so that the target wasn't seeing the same person, or people, constantly, which would become suspicious after a while.

Essentially, it would become a staggered conga line guided by radio.

Boyd continued walking at a regular pace along the footpath. The pedestrian traffic had become lighter, as the local citizens and other devout Muslims prepared for the approaching midday prayers.

The young soldier moved off from her position, staying on the other side of the road and back from Boyd. She kept relaying messages to update the location of the target.

"That's target across the road near Princess Tower…"

"Still moving west…"

"Target has crossed road, approaching the marina…"

All the while, Kryton manoeuvred the team via radio, either on foot or in the cars, into a position in order to covertly continue the follow. Although the radio chatter remained mostly formal, they were professional enough in their operations to talk plainly when needed.

"Jo, can you drop your people off at the north of the marina? We'll swap out Dingo Six."

"Yep. Moving now."

Jo exited her parked position and drove west along the inner roads, joining the vehicular traffic and manoeuvring into a location where she was able to drop off the two previously sleeping soldiers. To the common eye, it would simply have looked like two tourists exiting an uber. She then returned to the Tamani Hotel and retrieved Cav and Dalton.

Boyd then turned south, still following the edge of the waterfront of the Dubai Marina. He walked at a leisurely pace, as if he was a businessman on a long lunch break, or perhaps a tourist simply enjoying the sights on a long-overdue holiday.

He continued walking, constantly being monitored by the young surveillance team. Kryton was impressed with their discipline and skills. Their radio updates provided the appropriate level of detail, allowing the operation to be tracked and relayed back to Greyfin HQ.

Jonas' voice came across the satellite radio.

"UAV airborne. Expect it to be on-station in ninety minutes."

"Acknowledged. We've got sufficient coverage at this point on foot," Kryton replied.

At this point at least, he then thought to himself.

He knew that as long as Boyd remained on foot, they had sufficient manpower to watch him. However, Dubai was a dense urban environment, with multiple overlapping roads and plenty of side streets. If the target was to suddenly get into a vehicle and drive off – which trained intelligence operators would do if undertaking counter-surveillance actions – then he could just as quickly disappear into the local traffic.

That's why an eye in the sky would be helpful. Until then, however, Kryton would have to delicately find a balance between having the cars close enough to take up the follow if needed, but not so close that they looked like confused tourists sporadically pulling over and doing laps around the block. That could catch the attention of the local police.

Boyd continued walking, away from the marina and towards the busy Sheikh Zayed Road. He crossed a bridge, stopping for a moment and slightly turning back towards the way he had just come. He pulled the brochure from the paper and opened it up, which displayed a large map of the city.

Several people walked past him in either direction, going about their own business.

"This is Dingo Three. Have washed through target. He's stopped on the bridge and is looking at a map," reported the team member, meaning that he had deliberately continued walking past Boyd on the bridge as he had been close enough to maintain eyes on him, but too close to also stop suddenly when Boyd had.

Had he also suddenly have stopped, it would have been noticed as an unusual action by Boyd, who would have likely suspected something.

"Acknowledged," replied Kryton. "Dingo Two, you're up."

"Roger," said the next team member in line, who fastened his pace in order to get into a position to observe and follow the target.

Boyd continued his journey, completing his crossing of the bridge and entering the metro tram station. He stopped at the platform, looking at the timetable on the electronic board, and then at his watch.

The two surveillance operators were now also on the platform, both at separate ends and hidden amongst the people congregated and waiting for the next tram.

"Target is on the tram platform. Stationary," reported Dingo Two softly into his collar microphone whilst sitting on the bench and playing with his phone.

"For which direction?" asked Kryton.

The young team member looked up at the arrivals board. The LED readout flashed across the screen like a ticker tape.

Next Tram to City – 6 minutes.

"To the city," he said.

Kryton relayed the location to Canberra and then looked at Lewis. "Let's go," he said.

The young officer placed the Camry into drive and gently exited the carpark. Kryton radioed Jo, instructing her to get into a position on the main Sheikh Zayed Road so they could follow the tram, which ran on a line that was elevated on concrete pylons parallel to the main road.

The commuters waited as a tram moving in the opposite direction stopped momentarily at the station. Passengers made their exit, and upon the whistle from the station manager, it continued along its way.

A few minutes later, almost to the scheduled second, the city bound tram pulled up alongside the platform.

Dingo Two stepped onto the tram first – a deliberate act in case Boyd was conducting surveillance detection. Dingo Three remained stationary at the other end of the platform. A tourist group provided the perfect cover as he watched Boyd, who was still standing stationary.

"What's he doing?" asked Kryton, as Lewis slowly moved their car along the side roads, stopping briefly for Dingo Six to jump into the back, having hurriedly made her way to Kryton's location for a hasty pick-up.

"He's waiting," replied Dingo Two, who had taken a seat in the tram that allowed him to view the target standing on the platform looking aimlessly at the opened tram doors.

Dingo Three stayed still. His position was to the rear and away from Boyd. The tourist group had almost finished boarding the tram, and there was now a risk that the young soldier would be the only person left on the platform, apart from Boyd and the conductor.

That would make him stand out.

"Target still waiting. Should Dingo Three board?" asked Dingo Two, seeing what was happening from inside the tram.

The young soldier stepped forward two paces, and then eased up. He was now parallel to Boyd.

"Stand clear. Doors closing," came a voice over the loudspeaker.

The conductor blew his whistle, raising the white flag to signal to the tram driver that it was almost all clear for him to continue the journey.

"Sunray, does Three go?" asked the seated young soldier again.

Kryton's mind raced through the options available, and the possible consequences of each. He didn't want to compromise the operation. But he didn't want to lose Boyd, either. He would have loved to have had UAV support at that moment. It would have solved the issue instantly.

But as he had said earlier to Lewis, they would have to do this old school. And there were SOPs in place for that. They still knew where Boyd was, and for all intents and purposes, they had him boxed. Discretion would have to be the better part of valour.

"Board the tram," Kryton directed.

Dingo Three stepped forward, hopping onto the coat tails of the last tourist in the group and boarding the tram.

The doors started to close. Boyd leapt forward, turning his body sideways and knocking the doors as they closed. The Emirati conductor just frowned and shook his head, no doubt thinking it was another stupid westerner thinking the rules around public transport travel timings didn't apply to him.

Boyd stepped further into the interior of the tram, finding an aisle seat and sitting down, looking towards the front of the direction of travel.

"Target is on tram," Dingo Two whispered softly into his concealed radio.

Kryton exhaled as he looked at Lewis. The captain manoeuvred the car and drove towards the nearby entry onto the Sheikh Zayed Road, joining the flowing traffic and heading towards the main part of the city.

"Jo, what's your location?" he asked his fellow Greyfin team member.

"Just picked up Dingo's Four and Five. Moving towards the main road. Will be to your rear," replied Cav, sitting in the front seat next to Jo, whilst Dalton crammed into the rear with the other army team members.

"Ack," replied Kryton, as Lewis entered the on-ramp and drove onto the multi-laned main arterial road leading towards the major part of Dubai.

The sprawling skyscrapers bracketed the road, which continued up in front of them as far as the eye could see. The afternoon winds were starting to flare up, blanketing the sky in a thin layer of sand that significantly reduced visibility.

"There it is," he said, pointing to the tram speeding along the rail.

A few moments later, Jo also entered the Sheikh Zayed Road, racing through the traffic and getting within sight of Kryton's car.

"Sunray, we see you to our one-o'clock at fifty metres," said Cav over the radio.

Kryton tilted his head towards the rear-view mirror, spotting his team among the eclectic mix of vans, trucks, and luxurious sports cars often driven by the Emirati elite.

The two cars continued following the tram. Their job would be to get other team members into a position to continue the follow if and when Boyd exited the tram.

About a kilometre along the line, the tram pulled into the Al-Khail Metro station. As it slowed, Boyd stood from his seated position and moved towards the doors.

"Possible target movement off of tram," whispered Dingo Two into his mic.

"Roger. Three, you prepare to exit and follow from the front," instructed Kryton.

A double click on his PTT was sufficient enough a response for Kryton to know that the soldier understood. He looked closely at the maps, preparing to find the best routes off of the main road in order to get the other team members into a position to continue following Boyd. The roads of Dubai, although frequently busy, were conducive to rapid movement to and from the main roads.

A lack of any enforced speed limits would also assist the team to move around quickly.

The tram came to a complete stop. As planned, Dingo Three exited first, moving his way slowly across the platform and towards the exit of the station. He would be able to mingle amongst the passengers and find a secluded spot where he could swap out with one of the other vehicle-borne team members.

Dingo Two watched as Boyd took a step towards the tram's exit. He was about to get up when Boyd suddenly stopped.

The young soldier stopped, having the presence of mind to shift his body and pull his wallet from his back pocket, opening it and pretending to look for something whilst remaining seated.

He knew exactly what Boyd was doing.

He turned his head to look out the window, ensuring that he could still see Boyd, who was still standing on the tram. Several passengers exited and entered the tram. Boyd remained still, looking through the doors and onto the platform.

Less than a minute later, the conductor's whistle rang out, and the doors closed, with Boyd still standing inside the tram.

"This is Two. Target has *not* exited. I say again, *not* exited," he said softly into his mic whilst covering his mouth by pretending to scratch his face.

He watched as Boyd returned to his seat several rows in front of him and again facing the direction of travel.

Lewis looked at Kryton.

"Did he just conduct...?"

"He sure as shit did," replied Kryton, confirming the captain's theory that Boyd had just enacted a classic surveillance detection move.

By pretending to prepare to get off the tram, he had forced anyone following to make a decision as to whether to get off it first in anticipation of his exit. Doing so would reduce the chances of detection, as they would expect the target to be watching out for people *following* them off the tram.

The downside to such a move, however, was that once the surveillance operative had departed the tram, they were committed to the action. Any attempt to turn around and get back on the tram would be obvious, and would likely compromise the operatives and their actions.

Fortunately, Kryton had two people on the tram, so they were in a position to lose an operative by taking the risk. Unfortunately, however, he now knew that the target was actively looking for surveillance. They would have to be extra diligent in their actions, and look to swap people out as frequently as required to ensure Boyd wasn't seeing the same faces too often.

Dingo Three would have to catch the next tram and RV with the team at a later stage.

"All callsigns, this is Sunray. It's assessed as certain that target is conducting surveillance detection. Maintain discipline, and don't take any unnecessary risks."

Lewis raced around the block, having exited the Sheikh Zayed Road in anticipation of Boyd exiting the tram. Jo was now the lead car, with its complement of Australian soldiers and one lone SEAL. They continued following the tram as it continued its journey.

Kryton pulled up the previous day's surveillance log. He tracked the current movements of Boyd and compared them. They were almost identical.

"He's definitely conducting a wash," Kryton said. "It's almost exactly the same movements as yesterday. Did your team notice any counter-surveillance activity yesterday?"

"Nothing like what we're seeing now," she replied.

He jumped onto the satellite radio to talk to HQ.

"Jonas. Boyd is conducting a wash. I think he might be heading to a meet right now."

Jonas smiled as he stood in the ops centre looking at the digital maps that displayed several dots – the locations of each of the team members and their cars. What is known as Blue Force Tracking.

"Nice work, Sunray. This is what we were hoping for," he said.

"But why do it twice in two days?" Lewis asked Kryton.

"Could be a few reasons," replied Kryton. "Maybe he was conducting a rehearsal of his route to a meet; perhaps the meet was cancelled yesterday; and, it's possible he thought he was under surveillance yesterday, so now he's being more diligent as a result. Do you think the team was compromised?"

Lewis thought for a moment, trying to remember any specific events that might have suggested that her team had done something that had exposed them.

She shook her head as she weaved past some roadworks, and raced back onto the main road.

"No. I'm happy we kept a low profile. We didn't have eyes on him the entire time, but we're sure that he didn't meet anyone," she said confidently.

He couldn't help but continue to be impressed by her. She had been considered and honest in her answer. Ego had no place in the intelligence trade.

Unfortunately, the community could be full of it.

"So, where is he off to?" asked Kryton rhetorically, looking over the previous day's log.

He compared the notes and looked over the electronic map.

"Central Dubai most likely," suggested Lewis.

"Looks that way," he said in agreement with her.

Dingo Two continued updating Boyd's location as the two-car convoy followed the tram as it made several more stops as it progressed towards downtown Dubai. The target continued his journey, ostensibly oblivious to the presence of an Australian eye watching his every move. The young soldier reported that Boyd was texting on a mobile phone.

"Jonas, will the UAV have comms intercept capability?" asked Kryton.

"Affirmative. Time on station is fifty-minutes."

"That will come in handy, though it would be nice to have that now," lamented Kryton.

They approached Dubai Creek – a natural seawater inlet expanded through engineering that essentially made central Dubai a standalone island. Both cars crossed the bridge, remaining firmly behind the tram. Through the hazy skyline, they could now see the towering iconic skyscraper known as the Burj-Khalifa.

Suddenly, Dingo Two came across the radio.

"Possible bogeys near target," he said.

Kryton looked at Lewis. She looked as unsure about the call as he did.

He knew that the young surveillance operator wasn't in a position to say much without looking like a crazy person talking to themselves on public transport. He would assist Two to send details without having to say very much.

"Two. This is Sunray. How many?"

"Two of them," he replied.

"Male? Female? Both?"

"Both," he added.

"Interacting or nearby?"

"Nearby," he said.

"Send brief when can."

Dingo Two looked out of the window. He pulled out a map, opening it up and leaning forward in his seat, which helped to obscure his profile from the people nearby.

He talked softly but firmly.

"Male: Mid-thirties. Caucasian. White polo over khaki chinos, with a brown jacket. Female: Late-twenties. Mediterranean. Pink blouse over blue jeans," he reported, giving descriptions based off of a pre-determined briefing format.

Kryton wrote the details down.

"What's your thoughts?" he asked Two.

The soldier paused for a moment, cautiously examining the two people who had boarded a stop earlier and who had sat in adjacent seats several rows from Boyd.

He lowered his head again.

"They were at the hotel last night, in the restaurant," he said.

"Acknowledged, Two," said Kryton.

Kryton wasn't jumping to conclusions just yet. It would be perfectly natural to see people at a hotel and then again around town. The young surveillance operator was right to note it, though.

Kryton also knew that if the young operator had seen them before, then it made sense that they may also have seen him. If they were indeed doing something nefarious, then it made sense that they would also be on the lookout for anything unusual or threatening.

It was time to swap him out.

He looked at the map and found the approaching stations, and then pressed the PTT on the team radio.

"Jo, I'm pushing forward to Business Bay Metro. Can your car take over control?"

"We can," replied Cav from inside the nearby vehicle.

Kryton looked over his shoulder to Dingo Six sitting in the back seat. He raised his eyebrows enthusiastically at the young woman.

"Ready to go for a walk?"

18

Lewis floored the accelerator, weaving in between traffic and racing towards the turnoff that would allow Kryton and Dingo Six to disembark at the upcoming busy tram station. Their assessment was that Boyd would likely leave the tram there, based on the movements he had conducted previously. However, they had been very recently wrong in making assumptions, so they would have to remain vigilant.

Jo and her band of operators remained firmly crammed in their own car, keeping pace with the tram just in case Boyd decided to get off at one of the smaller stations prior to Business Bay.

"Geez, it's a bit tight in here. You two been taking steroids?" Dalton said sarcastically to the two stocky Australian intelligence operators sitting on either side of him.

One of the young soldiers looked at the frogman, who was rather well built himself.

"We've been eating lots of protein whilst deployed," retorted Dingo Four.

"Ah, I see. What type?" asked the American, unconvinced.

"Mostly seal," deadpanned Dingo Five with a perfectly timed use of a double meaning.

Dalton's jaw hung loose for a moment. He went to rebuke their comments, but he had no words. He exhaled deeply and closed his mouth, folding his arms and looking straight ahead with wounded pride.

In the battle of wits and patronising humour, it was Australia – 1. US – 0.

Jo looked over to the giggling mess in the passenger seat next to her, where Cav was trying to stop himself from completely losing it. He turned his head to look at his special forces colleague. Dalton just continued scowling.

Back in the lead car, a more serious tone continued to play out. Lewis skillfully manoeuvred past some roadwork and managed to make the exit ramp. She raced around to the side road, pulling in behind some taxis.

"The northeast exit is closed off for repairs," she exclaimed gleefully.

Kryton smiled. This meant that there were less egress routes they would have to cover.

"Push forward towards the town centre. RV with Jo and even out the numbers in the cars," he said to her as they came to a complete stop.

"Roger," she replied, as the two intelligence operators exited the car.

As quickly as they had arrived, Lewis was gone, re-joining the bustling afternoon traffic.

Kryton nodded at Dingo Six as they enacted their doctrinal drills, walking towards the station proper and finding naturally concealed positions by where they could observe the exiting passengers.

As was typical in Dubai, the noise of the traffic intermingled with the cacophony of building construction – the repercussion of a city that still hadn't worked out what it wanted to look like.

The busy metro station had several exits. People could either exit the tram and walk downstairs on the same side as the platform, or they could cross the overpass towards the shops on the other side of the main road.

Kryton stopped and thought for a few seconds. They knew that Boyd was conducting surveillance detection, so he had to ask himself: what would *he* do in Boyd's shoes? He walked around the front of the terminal and found Dingo Six nestled near a bus stop.

"Position yourself in this equivalent location, but over there," he said, pointing to the base of the overpass on the other side of the road.

Dingo Six nodded, then raced up the stairs and towards her new location.

The noise of a motor descending in pitch gained Kryton's attention, and he looked up to see the tram slowly pulling into the station. He moved to join several middle-eastern and south-Asian taxi drivers huddled around a car, and even managed to get one of them to give him a cigarette.

Dingo Two continued to provide updates as the tram came to a complete halt. Then there was silence on the radio. Every team member, spread across the nearby area, listened intently.

It felt like ages. The passengers had already started to disembark. It was a large crowd, and Kryton knew that even in such close confines, it was still possible to lose a target.

Just as he was about to demand an update, Dingo Two spoke.

"Target off. Target off. Bogeys have followed," he briefed, giving as much information as he could.

"Roger," replied Kryton. "We'll take the follow."

"Acknowledged. Dingo Two off follow," said the soldier, as he watched the doors close nearby to his seat, remaining firmly in it as the tram started to move off.

His job was done for now.

Kryton and his counterpart stayed in their positions, waiting to see where Boyd would go. They were equally as curious to see which direction the two new people in the unfolding saga would walk.

It was still uncertain who they were. It was quite possible that they were a young couple enjoying the sights of the city. Until that had been proven otherwise, however, they would be viewed suspiciously.

Kryton watched the gaggle of people walk down the stairs from the platform and off in every direction. He was closer to the station exit on his side of the overpass than Dingo Six was on her side, so if Boyd was coming in his direction, he would see him first.

"Nothing seen my side," said Dingo Six through the radio.

"That's because he's walking across the street from me," said Kryton, announcing to the team that he was now leading the follow of the suspected assassin.

The experienced Australian intelligence operator held firm for a moment, as Boyd turned 180 degrees after exiting the station and started walking along the footpath parallel to it and towards the city.

His suspicions we correct. The two bogeys also existed only a few moments later, and just as Boyd had done, they also turned 180 degrees and walked on the footpath alongside the station.

All his years of experience suggested that there was something about them that didn't feel quite right. Something hard to articulate, but a feeling that only comes with time and experience.

He would remain very cautious of them.

"Dingo Six, come back across to my side and become my tail," he said to his colleague.

"Roger."

Kryton quickly bid farewell to his new found friends, extinguishing the cigarette with his foot and swiftly jogging across the road, not taking his eye off of Boyd for a second.

Meanwhile, Jo and her packed car made their way to a side road towards the city, where they would be in a position to drop off some of the surveillance team to support Kryton and Dingo Six. The pedestrian and road traffic was starting to make it difficult to maintain good optics on the targets, so it would be crucial that they had every available operator supporting the effort.

Lewis was similarly dealing with the traffic, rushing around to try and recover Dingo Two and Three.

Kryton was comfortable in the follow, watching as Boyd proceeded along the footpath, still parallel to the Sheikh Zayed Road. Suddenly, the target pivoted on his toes and ran across the road, looking over his shoulder to look out for and avoid oncoming traffic.

The move also gave him the opportunity to look back in the direction he had been walking, without being too obvious about it.

Another classic surveillance detection tactic.

However, there was always a counter to the counter.

Kryton kept moving in the direction of travel, still remaining far enough back to see Boyd, who had now made it across the road and was again walking in the same direction.

Dingo Six gently made her way across the road to be on the same side as Boyd, using a delivery truck slowly moving along the road as concealment for her action.

Boyd then made a right turn and headed up a side road which bracketed a small group of shops.

Kryton gave directions into his covert microphone as Dingo Six continued after Boyd. He watched as the two bogeys also suddenly made a right turn just as Boyd had turned down the side street.

What started as a suspicion suddenly turned to almost certainty.

The way they had moved clearly indicated that they were also following Boyd.

But why?

"All callsigns, this is Sunray. Designator for bogeys is now bandits," said Kryton.

This meant that he now firmly believed that the man and woman were now involved in some way with Boyd, and were not just a couple of tourists incidentally nearby. Until it could be determined exactly who they were, and what their intentions were, they would be viewed as a real-time threat to the operation.

"Dingo Six. Hold your position and attempt covert image capture of the bandits. Utilise descriptions as previously indicated," he added.

"Roger."

Kryton turned and also crossed the street. It was once again a conga line of stakeholders, but with some new additions. Boyd at the front, followed roughly two dozen metres behind by Dingo Six. About a similar distance behind the female Australian were the two bandits, and then behind them was Kryton. All mingled amongst the afternoon crowds. Dingo Six veered away from the follow and pulled out her mobile phone, finding an inconspicuous position where she could obtain a photo of the two bandits.

"Cav, get onto Jonas and see if there are any other elements operating in this area. We need to know who these people are."

"Roger. On it now," replied Cav, hanging onto his seat as Jo tore around the side streets to get into a position to drop some of the team off.

Cav communicated back to Canberra, where Jonas ordered his analysts to get on the phones to contact their many liaison officers in the intelligence and special operations entities globally.

"Get Langley. Get Whitehall...even chase down INTERPOL," he instructed them.

Dingo Six managed to obtain a decent image of the man and woman, sending the image back to Cav, who was then able to send it in encrypted form back to Canberra. The images then appeared on the large screen in the Greyfin ops room.

Who are you two, I wonder? Jonas thought to himself, loosening his necktie and wiping his brow.

"Sir, Langley states that they have no teams in the area," said one of the US analysts.

"JSOC says the same," added another one.

Jonas just nodded.

"Assume they are not friendlies," he said to the team in Dubai.

Kryton continued to follow them on foot, through the Bay Avenue Mall, into an open-air market, and then towards the waterfront which sat at the base of the sprawling Burj Khalifa building. The mixture of western shops and Arabian culture intertwined like an incongruous symphony that somehow worked.

The scent of coffee and perfume reminded Kryton of the few days immediately after the conclusion of many long deployments inside Iraq and Afghanistan, where Australian soldiers were given leave in Dubai before returning home. The sights, smells, and sounds of the Emirati city were in vast contrast to those experienced by most of the soldiers whilst on operations.

123

There was no time for nostalgia now, however. He continued passing updates to the team, who had now moved into various positions in anticipation of Boyd's movements.

Kryton soon approached a small footbridge, which sat at the base and in the shadow of the magnificent towering structure. The Dubai fountain shot into the air to his right, making for a beautiful sight for the happy snapping tourists, but making it difficult for Kryton to manoeuvre around them on the narrow overpass.

He needn't have worried about losing sight of Boyd or the other two, though.

"This is Cav. I'm with Jo. We've got the target and are in follow. Bandits are still on his six," came a reassuring voice through the radio.

The two Aussies had made haste to manoeuvre their car through the confined streets surrounding the popular tourist area, and then get into a position to intercept Boyd on foot.

Surveillance teams often felt like seagulls busily following a fishing boat at sea – always moving and hoping to be in the right place at the right time, anticipating the next movement.

Like free fish for the seagulls, however, the reward for their patience and hard work would be the intelligence they would be able to gather.

19

Cav and Jo continued to follow Boyd, who proceeded along the waterfront and into the Dubai Mall. The huge shopping hub was one of the largest completely covered buildings in the world, and the air-conditioning provided relief from the early afternoon Dubai heat.

The two Australians fitted in perfectly amongst the eclectic crowd, and to the naked eye, they were just another western couple walking around town.

Kryton veered off and took a seat by a large palm tree, where a Japanese couple was trying to capture the perfect memory on their iPhone.

"Clay, what's your loc?" he asked.

The American had also left the car to the young Dingo operators when Cav and Jo had exited it, and had made his way inside the mall.

"Standing by near the Gold Souk."

Kryton thought for a moment, visualising where everyone was in relation to their target. The bandits were still a concern, so he decided to allow Cav and Jo to watch Boyd, and he would link with Clay to cover the man and woman. He would also bring a few of the soldiers in to be ready to take over the follow, just in order to have some redundancy.

Meanwhile, back in Canberra, Jonas and the supporting team were busily analysing the images that had been sent to them. The quality wasn't bad for a smartphone, but the satellite connection had made them a bit grainy. The analysts were busily trying to determine who the people in the images might actually be. The benefit of having all available resources was that they could tap into almost any database available, whether it be to check on a driver's licence or a mugshot from a criminal record.

The supercomputers at NSA were now being worked overtime in an attempt to identify the bandits.

Cav and Jo followed Boyd into the main entrance of the mall, where he walked past the currency exchanges and banks, and towards the area with the restaurants. They were soon near an English themed pub, and they watched as Boyd entered it and took a seat at the front bar. It was about half full, with the tourists and business people alike in the final stages of eating their lunch.

They casually followed him inside, finding a spare table across the other side of the pub. The bandits then entered the bar less than a minute later, also finding a table, but closer to the back wall, where they sat down and placed some of their personal possessions in front of them, as if preparing to settle in.

Kryton and Dalton took a few minutes to link up, and then proceeded to enter a café several shops down and across the other side of the mall. From their position, they would easily be able to view the front of the pub.

Boyd pulled some items out of his inner pockets, placing them down on the bar as the waiter approached him to take his order. He ordered a Heineken, which the waiter poured from the long tap. Beads of condensation trickled down the side of the glass as he took a sip.

Cav looked over to the bandit's table. They sat there looking at the menu, occasionally looking up and over at Boyd.

"They're definitely looking at him?" he said quietly to Jo, whilst also pressing the PTT on his mic to allow Kryton and Dalton to hear the commentary.

Kryton considered the situation. The bandits were following Boyd – of that he was certain. But did Boyd know that they were? If he was conducting surveillance detection, then he might also have noticed them for a second time in two days, just as the young soldier had on the tram.

He decided to make an executive decision.

"Cav. Jo. Check his reaction to a bump on the bandits," he instructed his colleagues.

Cav looked up at Jo and smiled.

"Guess we better play the part," he said, standing up and walking over to the bar, deliberately staying a reasonable distance from Boyd.

"Two Heinekens, please mate," he said to the waiter behind the bar.

The man smiled and nodded, and as he had done for Boyd, poured two glasses of cold beer. Cav looked at them eagerly. There had to be some perks to the job, after all!

He paid in Dirhams – the local currency of the U.A.E. – and then proceeded back to the table.

This time, he walked past the bandits.

Just as he got within the right distance, he pretended to trip.

He dropped the glasses onto the floor, spilling beer over the thick woollen carpet as well as onto the table, where the bandits instinctively jumped up, trying to avoid getting any of the amber fluid onto their clothes. Cav embellished the 'accident', deliberately reaching out to knock their belongings onto the floor under the guise of trying to catch the glasses. The commotion caused the pub-goers to turn their heads to see what the fuss was all about.

All except for Jo.

She kept her eyes firmly on Boyd, looking to see what his reaction was. If he knew he was under surveillance from the bandits, he might take the opportunity to sneak away whilst they were distracted. If he didn't, then he might stay in place and watch the unfolding drama, assuming it was just a noisy and unrelated accident.

He did neither. Instead, he just looked ahead at the mirrored wall in front of him, which housed the myriad of spirits and other assorted pub type paraphernalia. Jo watched as he simply took a sip of his beer, before folding his newspaper up and placing his glass down on top of it.

Cav was now on his knees, ostensibly trying to pick up the possessions of the clearly annoyed bandits, but in reality, looking through the items as he manhandled them to see if there was anything of interest.

"I'm so sorry. That's completely my mistake," he said as he clumsily rummaged through their items.

The woman bent down, grabbing her small handbag, and quickly trying to put items back into it.

"Just leave it. It's okay," she said, in what sounded like an English accent.

The man also kneeled down, pulling his jacket out of the liquid mess. Cav reached out to help him up, briefly noticing something on the man's hip as his white polo lifted up ever so slightly.

It was a concealed holster, and inside it, a pistol.

He quickly averted his gaze, pretending not to notice it. He then grabbed the man's jacket, continuing to play the clown.

"Mate, I'm sorry, let me help you up," he said, as he firmly grabbed the man by the arm and lifted him up to his feet. The waiter had come over with a cloth and started to help clean up the mess. Another also came over, guiding the couple to a fresh table nearby.

"I'll get some new beers for you, sir," he said to Cav politely.

A small item slipped from the male bandit's jacket pocket as he shook it off whilst trying to brush the beer off of it. Cav looked down, then reached down to pick it up.

It was an Australian passport.

Cav looked at it, then looked at the man.

"You're Aussies!?" he stated, trying to hide what was actual surprise and a little bit of confusion.

The man nodded, looking agitated and checking on his partner.

"Yes, we are," he replied. "Look, it is fine. Don't worry about it," he added, still brushing some of the beer off of his clothing.

Cav pulled the chair out for the woman, who reluctantly smiled as she sat down. The man also took his seat. Cav offered a few more platitudes as he attempted to quickly open the document to get the man's name. He was too slow, however, and the man grabbed it off of him before he could sneak a look.

"We're fine. Thank you. You can go now," said the man dismissively.

Cav stepped back a pace and smiled at them as he continued to apologise. He slowly moved his way back to where Jo was sitting and re-joined her, then looked up and saw that the waiter had poured two new beers for them.

Jo was about to ask him what happened, but a moment of inspiration hit the special forces operator. He jumped up and walked to the bar, but not before stopping at the table where the bandit couple were sitting.

"Look, I'm sorry once again. You know it's not like us Aussies to not buy a beer spilt in a pub, so please let me buy you two one each," he said to them hopefully.

The man looked at Cav and nodded, perhaps more as a means to ensure that they would be left alone than in acceptance of the kind offer. He was about to continue to the bar, before looking down at the woman.

"Oh, I was wondering if you might know how many goals Shane Warne kicked for the Canberra Raiders in the footy last night? I'm a big fan, but we couldn't get the scores from our hotel," he said.

She looked up at Cav, appearing lost for words, before stuttering an answer.

"No, I don't... I mean, we don't," she replied in a manner much friendlier than her counterpart.

"Okay, no worries. I'll get those beers."

Cav walked to the bar, retrieving his own drinks and placing an order for the couple, before returning to Jo. He covertly pressed his PTT button to update his Greyfin colleagues, who had been able to observe some of the calamitous action from their own seats in the café adjacent to the pub.

"They're carrying Aussie passports, but they're definitely not Aussies," he said.

"Are you completely sure?" asked Kryton.

"Positive. I did the Warney kicking goals test. The bloke's accent is pretty average, too."

Dalton looked across at Kryton with a confused look.

"It's like asking an American how many touchdowns Babe Ruth scored for the Dallas Cowboys. Even non-sports lovers would know it's a stupid question," Kryton informed the SEAL about Cav's quick nationality test to the bandits in the pub.

"Ah, fair enough," said Dalton, giving an amused smile.

Cav and Jo maintained their cover, sitting in their seats and appearing to be a couple enjoying their day out, all the while keeping an eye on Boyd. Their target sat at the bar, occasionally looking at his watch.

The waiter delivered the tray of beers to the bandit's table. Cav raised his glass and winked at them; a gesture reluctantly reciprocated.

"I'll knock your fucking head off," mumbled Cav as he took a sip from his beer, still smiling.

Jo looked at him, unimpressed by his aggressive attitude, but one that she had become unaccustomed to from working with special forces operators previously.

Suddenly, Lewis' voice came on the radio.

"Sunray. This is One. Jonas has sent the following: intercept and detain target."

Dalton sat a little more upright in his chair and gave Kryton a small nod. He brushed his hand over his hip – allowing himself the peace of mind that came with confirming his weapon was ready to go if needed.

"Acknowledged. All callsigns, await my instructions," he replied.

"How do we do it?" asked Dalton.

Kryton looked across at the pub, his mind racing as to the courses of action available to him. He mentally considered the battlespace, working out where his people were and the best positions to place them.

He jumped onto the radio and received a complete location status. Most of the team were nearby in support, except for Lewis who was closing in on the location after having retrieved the two surveillance operators who had been on the tram.

He was comfortable that Boyd was surrounded. It was now a matter of waiting for the opportune moment. It would have to be somewhere not too visible to the public. Normally, that sort of snatch and grab needed to be well planned, specifically rehearsed, and conducted at a place and time typically of their own choosing. Nothing within the current situation afforded that.

But this was what Greyfin had been formed for – to undertake the difficult missions in the most complex situations.

A few minutes went by, and Boyd finished his drink. He got up from his seat and put a few coins from his pocket onto the counter.

"Standby. Possible target movement," said Cav.

Boyd walked to the exit of the pub, stopping and observing the passing shoppers for a moment. He scratched his forehead, then turned around and walked to the back of the bar. It was deep enough into the pub that Kryton lost sight of him.

"Where's he going?" he asked across the comms network.

"Looks like the bathroom," whispered Jo in reply.

Kryton looked at Dalton, who returned the uneasy gaze. The toilet of a pub was hardly the best place to make the takedown, but losing sight of the target didn't feel much better. They waited.

One minute turned into two. And then three.

Kryton restrained himself from getting up.

Patience was the key. There was an armed element sitting in the same pub as his team, and their intentions were still unclear. If they provoked anything too soon, who knows what could happen. The armed bandits may choose not to be as discreet as Kryton's team.

A large cracking noise pierced their ears, causing both Kryton and Dalton to slightly jump. They both heard random noises in their earpieces, followed by a moment of static before it went quiet again.

"This is Sunray. What's happening?" asked Kryton.

The radio sat silent for a moment, before a groaning voice spoke.

"This is Dingo Five. I'm down," it said, the pain and agony of a clearly injured surveillance operator obvious to all of them.

Kryton looked at Dalton wide-eyed, then over at the pub.

"Fuck. Boyd."

He jumped up and ran across the mall, darting in between the shoppers. He raced into the pub at a fast walk, conscious to not alert the bandits that something was up. Cav and Jo watched as he walked straight to the rear where the bathrooms were. He drew his weapon. Discretion was a fluid concept anyway.

He booted the door of the male bathroom open, raising his weapon to eye level. He entered, finding it completely empty. He checked the main stalls. Also empty.

He turned to leave the room and saw Dalton standing at the door. The SEAL had worked out what Kryton was doing.

"Female bathrooms and kitchen also empty," said the American.

Kryton walked out of the bathroom and into a service corridor. Dalton followed. They saw several boxes and crates of empty bottles. They went around the corner and saw a fire escape with its door slightly ajar. The alarm had been deliberately disconnected.

"Shit," muttered Kryton, pushing the door open and exiting outside into an alley at the back of the massive mall.

The two men ran a couple of dozen metres to the side of an industrial bin, where a prone body was lying incapacitated on the ground.

It was one of the young soldiers.

Dalton kneeled down, conducting a quick assessment of the injured digger. Apart from a bloody nose and a possible concussion, he would be fine. The SEAL looked up at Kryton.

"He got worked over pretty good, but he'll live."

Kryton looked at the well-built and perfectly capable soldier.

He must have some skills, he thought to himself about the way Boyd had easily dealt with one of his team members. He looked up to the end of the alley, about fifty metres away. He raced up to the end, where it opened up onto the waterfront again.

There were people everywhere, scattered in all directions. Boyd could have gone anywhere.

"Cav, Boyd's got away out the back," he said into his mic.

Back inside the pub, the bandits had made a hasty exit. Cav and Jo waited a moment for them to leave, then jumped up and also exited, seeking to get into a position to inconspicuously follow them.

"We're on the bandits, mate. They're in a hurry out of the pub," replied Cav.

Kryton ran back to Dalton, who had heard the update from Cav.

"I think it's safe to say we're compromised," he said to the Australian.

"He must have got spooked in the pub," said Kryton. "Get some of the others and look after him. I'll back up Cav. Maybe the two intruders can explain what just happened."

"Copy that," said Dalton.

Kryton started running back towards to fire escape of the pub. He spoke into his radio.

"Cav. Don't let them get away."

20

Cav and Jo bristly walked out of the pub and into the main part of the mall. The bandits were at least thirty metres away, walking away quickly.

"Shit. Let's move it," exclaimed Cav to Jo.

The two Australians quickened the pace, and by the time they reached the corner of the row of shops, they were practically jogging. As they turned the corner, they could see the man and woman still hurriedly walking away, crossing to the other side of the aisle to the front of the various high-end clothing stores.

The male bandit looked over his shoulder, making direct eye contact with Cav. The look on the commando's face showed clear intent. The man said something to his companion, and she too looked over her shoulder to see their pursuers.

The two of them started running. Cav and Jo rushed to follow, manoeuvring in between the daytime shoppers and keeping their eyes firmly on their new targets.

Several shoppers looked on curiously, wondering why there were several westerners sprinting across the marble floors of the luxurious goods area of the mall.

Cav and Jo struggled to keep up, having to weave in-between the shoppers and the island stands that sold clothing accessories or gave out tourist information. The bandits showed no such courtesy, knocking over several shoppers and spilling their bounty of designer handbags, brand name clothing, and other expensive goods.

A mall security guard blew his whistle – a fruitless attempt to stop the chase, and one that was completely ignored anyway. The Australians persevered, maintaining a visual view of the bandits whilst working their way through the retail themed obstacle course.

The chase continued through the mall, soon turning from a sprint and into a middle-distance event, highlighting just how big the shopping precinct actually was.

Slowly, Cav and Jo closed the gap – all those sand runs on the Gold Coast beaches finally paying off. The bandits realised it too, looking over their shoulders and trying to change their direction rapidly to confuse the Australians. They darted through an exit door and down a long corridor, leading away from the shops. Cav and Jo burst through; their eyes steeled with resolve. If they were going to catch them in a manner with any sort of discretion, it would have to be now.

The man and woman reached the end of the corridor, slowing enough in an attempt to push on the fire escape door.

It was locked.

The woman turned to see Cav and Jo, now side by side, literally within spitting distance of them. She started to run again, moving along the edge of the wall with the fire escape and heading towards a loading dock. Her companion had no such time. He went to withdraw his pistol from his concealed hip holster.

"Get her," Cav shouted, as he launched his body into the man. The male bandit wore the force of the special forces soldier's momentum, which knocked the pistol from his hand before he had a chance to raise it against the Australian.

Jo didn't need to be told twice. She turned the corner like a well-tuned rollercoaster, losing virtually no momentum as she did so. The woman attempted to increase her speed, but a tap into her back by Jo knocked her from her centre of gravity. Her legs stumbled over each other. She attempted to recover, but Jo closed the gap completely, grabbing her by her blouse and pulling her down by the shoulder. The woman crumpled into a heap on the ground, somersaulting before crashing into a bollard at the edge of the loading dock.

Cav had also fallen to the ground – the result of crashing into his opponent like a car at the demolition derby. He quickly got to his feet, turning to face the man who had also regained his balance. Meanwhile, Jo had attempted to throw herself onto the woman, who kicked out at her hip, forcing the Australian back and giving the female bandit enough time to stand up again.

It was now man versus man, woman versus woman.

Jo manoeuvred around her opponent, cutting off any escape. Cav did likewise, forcing his opponent against the wall. The two would have to fight their way through the Australians if they were to have any hope of escaping.

The male bandit struck first, launching a flurry of punches at Cav. The Australian easily blocked them, but he was surprised at the ferocity and power behind them from a man smaller in size and stature. He stepped back to open some space, before snapping his leg forward, kicking the man in the upper thigh and following it up with two severe blows with his right hand to the man's body, forcing him to buckle over.

Jo, on the other hand, struck her opponent first, landing a sweet left jab to the woman's face. She followed it up with a right cross, which knocked the bandit into the wall. With her confidence high, Jo attempted a solid kick to the lower part of the stomach, but the woman skilfully stepped to the side, and Jo's kick glanced off of her and harmlessly into the wall. The woman then countered, attempting a right hook at Jo's head. Fortunately for the Australian, her opponent wasn't close enough for it to land properly, and the blow merely brushed across the side of her face.

Both pairs continued attempting to get the upper hand, making attack and counter attack, and moving around each other like boxers in a title fight.

The male bandit decided that he wouldn't be able to win a standing match, so he launched himself at Cav's lower body. The Aussie commando attempted a counter, but the speed of his opponent's shoot was too quick. The two men went onto the ground, with Cav on his back. He grasped any part of the man's body that he could, doing anything to avoid being put into a submissive position. The man's skills were now concerning Cav. He had seen this type of fighting before, and even trained back at 2nd Commando Regiment in Sydney on the soft floor using some of these techniques. This man knew what he was doing.

Jo was experiencing the same ferocity and talent from her own opponent, and was struggling to get the upper hand, desperately countering a suite of violent blows to her upper body.

It was at that moment that she was grateful for all the hand-to-hand training Kryton had made the team undertake during their formation. She remembered the keywords he had told her: there's no such thing as a fair fight.

With that in mind, she stepped to the side to parry another blow from the woman, before reaching to grasp the back of her hair and pulling down on it sharply. This forced the woman's head back, and she let out a pitiful cry. Jo vigorously shook the woman's head from side to side, forcing her knees to buckle. This allowed Jo to move in closer to her, and he drove her right thumb into the inside of the woman's right eye.

The noise the woman made was earth-shattering, as Jo twisted her thumb inside the eye socket. The woman's body went limp. Jo

135

maintained the initiative, kneeing the hapless bandit in the back of the head, before removing the thumb and driving her fist across the woman's jaw, knocking her out.

Jo released her grip to let the unconscious body fall to the floor, standing back and kneeling over on her haunches. She was panting heavily. She looked down at the woman, lying prone and lifeless. The spluttering noise made from oxygen passing through a mouth full of blood indicated to Jo that the woman was still alive. She stood up, trying to comprehend how she was capable of such violence.

She didn't have time to dwell on that now, however. She looked a few metres away and saw Cav and the man engaged in a vicious grappling duel.

She drew her pistol as she walked over to them.

"Cav, roll off," she said firmly.

Cav tilted his head and saw Jo standing nearby with her pistol. He pulled his opponent in tightly and twisted his hips, rolling from his ground position and over onto his front, taking the man with him. He continued rolling towards Jo, pushing himself off of the man in order to separate them. The two fighters were now apart, and Jo moved in between the both of them.

She pointed her weapon straight at the man's head.

"Don't. Fucking. Move."

Cav turned over and rested on his knees. Apart from a few pieces of missing skin, he was otherwise okay. The intensity of the fight had taken it out of him. He was puffing like an old goat, much to his own chagrin.

He quickly composed himself, getting to his feet and moving back towards the man, pulling on his arm and flipping him onto his front.

"If you move, she *will* shoot you," he said in-between breaths.

"Are you alright?" he then asked Jo.

She nodded, still breathing heavily, but this time from the shock of combat.

"It's okay. Just breathe," he said to her reassuringly.

She took a long, deep breath, composing herself.

"I'm good," she said, nodding at Cav.

He looked around, seeing if anyone had seen what had just unfolded. They were still alone.

"Zach, we've detained two bandits. We need you here right away," he said into his radio, which through some miracle had not been damaged in the fight.

136

Cav cued Kryton onto their current location. Jo moved over to where he was standing, a few paces from the bandits.

"Who are they? She knew how to fight," exclaimed Jo.

Cav nodded in agreement.

"They both did. That was classic Krav Maga."

Fuck me, she thought to herself.

Although in a relatively concealed area, Cav knew that they had to find somewhere even less conspicuous. He ran around to the loading dock and found what appeared to be a disused storage room nestled into a culvert at the end of the bay. He found the light and switched it on. A dull glow from a single struggling globe lit the room sufficiently enough to see inside. Several tins of old paint and empty boxes sat on a table. Along with it was some old rope he was confident he could use to good effect.

He returned to where Jo was standing and leaned down to tie the man's hands behind his back. He then picked the man up, guiding him to a chair in the empty room, and securing him to a pipe on the wall with the rope. He then helped Jo carry the still unconscious woman into the same room, also tying her hands up and securing her to the pipe on the wall as well.

A few moments later, Kryton found them, bringing one of the soldiers with him. Cav explained what had happened. Kryton then gave them an update on what had happened outside of the pub.

"Will the kid be okay?" asked Cav.

"Yeah, he'll live. He'll just be a bit sore for a few days."

Kryton and Cav stood outside of the room for a moment, reviewing what had happened and attempting to join all the pieces together. They had the young soldier take a facial image of the two bandits, and then go to RV with Lewis and send the encrypted images back to Canberra for further assessment. They were certain that the clearer images would end up in the supercomputers of the NSA, which could draw upon multiple databases in order to try and find a match.

Jo had managed to source some water, splashing it over the woman's face, rousing her. The defeated female looked up at her assailant looking victoriously back down at her.

Outside, Kryton and Cav continued to try and ascertain what had happened.

How had Boyd escaped?

Well, that was simple. He legged it out the back door of the pub and smashed a poor army surveillance operator in the process.

Had he noticed the army surveillance team earlier?

Possibly; but they had kept some pretty tight drills during the follow.

Maybe it was the bandits that spooked him?

Perhaps; but who were they? And what was their role in all of this?

Kryton analysed the information at hand, taking a close look at the confiscated pistols of the two bandits – two identically matching Beretta Model 70s.

He knew that the storeroom wasn't ideal for an interrogation, as there was too high a risk of compromise. However, until they could find a way to extract their two detainees, they would have to sit tight. The shopping centre was still too crowded.

Kryton paced outside. He was nervous. Not only because of the precarious situation, but because of the suspicions he was starting to form in his head about the identities of the bandits.

Their skills. Their weapons. Their tactics.

Thirty long minutes later, Lewis came over the radio and passed on the details that had been sent from Jonas. The Greyfin analysts had been working overtime, and had made a crude, but highly confident, assessment of who the detainees were.

Kryton listened intently through his earpiece. Jo, guarding the two detainees in the room, and Cav, standing next to Kryton, listened also.

Cav looked at Kryton.

"Oh, fuck me," he said softly to his mate.

Kryton just sighed.

"Acknowledged. Dingo One, seek extraction options through HQ for two detainees," he instructed.

He looked at Cav in a manner that suggested it would be easier to just accept what they were fairly sure was true. He walked into the storeroom, approaching the man tied to the chair by the wall. He pulled one of those metallic fold-out chairs from between a cupboard, turning it around and sitting on it backwards, leaning on the backrest.

He looked straight at the man, observing the bruises starting to form on his face after his encounter with Cav. He then looked at the woman, who also looked the worse for wear thanks to Jo.

Kryton moved the chair slightly, enough so that he was facing both of the bandits.

"Tell me," he said softly whilst leaning in. "What is the Mossad doing in Dubai?"

Zach Kryton will be back…

Please feel free to follow us on social media and provide recommendations and feedback!

INSTAGRAM
joshfrancis_red.diamond

FACEBOOK
joshfrancisbooks

INSTAGRAM

FACEBOOK

AMAZON

Please leave an honest review on Amazon. This helps to tailor better content and allows for reader interaction.

Sign up to the readers group

Biography

Josh Francis qualified as high school teacher before commissioning into the Royal Australian Navy as a junior officer soon after the September 11 attacks in the US. A desire to serve on warlike operations saw him resign his commission and enlist into the Australian Army. After qualifying as an infantryman and paratrooper, Josh deployed on peacekeeping operations in Timor-Leste conducting counter-militia operations.

After completing basic and specialist intelligence operations training, Josh completed multiple deployments to Afghanistan and Iraq, conducting duties in conventional and special operations, as well as training roles.

He is the author of the military themed personal development books *The Camouflage Series*, as well as the *Zach Kryton* series of books. His debut book is titled *Under the Pump*, a memoir about his youthful antics whilst working at a petrol station in his hometown of Adelaide.

www.ingramcontent.com/pod-product-compliance
Lightning Source LLC
Chambersburg PA
CBHW070336130626
46556CB00007B/2884